Prolo

It was the autumn of eighteen sixty-three, the leaves on the trees were only starting to change from their faded green colour to their deep sunset orange and were scantily scattered on the ground.

Emily Jones loved this time of year.

She and her sister Hyacinth loved to walk under the canopy of the oak trees and ponder on what life lay ahead for them both. What self-respecting thirteen year old didn't think about things to come at that age? Hyacinth was walking behind Emily kicking leaves about and generally enjoying her mid-afternoon walk. It wasn't cold and there was just a slight breeze whistling through the waves of branches.

"Come along Hyacinth, father will be cross with us if we are not back in time to help mother with the cooking."

"Oh Emily", came the eleven-year olds reply, as she picked up a handful of dead leaves and threw them in the direction of her older sister. "You worry too much, you know father won't be that cross with us", still came her sisters stern reply.

"I'd rather not take that chance, so come on we need to get home."

Georgette Jones was busy wringing out the last of the dirty water from her daughters clothes when finally the two of them came back. "Hello mother" came the cheeky grin of Hyacinth, "we are home now." Georgette looked up to see her two daughters standing in front of her. "Hyacinth Jones, look at the dirt on your dress."

Hyacinth glanced down at the soggy brownish material that weighed heavily on her legs.

"I am sorry mother, but we were playing in the leaves in the woods."

Emily glanced down at her younger sister and realised that the leaves that she was so happy playing in must have been damp and sodden.

"Go in at once and change that dress before father gets home, you know how particular he is."

Hyacinth said ok before skipping off into the wooden lodge to get changed.

"What time is father coming home?" Emily asked her mother, who by now had an arm full of wet washing that she had just finished sorting.

"He will be home within the hour, so we will need to get a move on and prepare his supper."

"OK mother I will go wash up and then start preparing for fathers arrival."

Both mother and daughter made their way into the small wooden lodge to start preparing supper for the family.

Henry Jones decided that it was enough for the day and began the arduous walk back to his cabin. It was hard work walking around the forest all day maintaining the wooden fence that meandered around the outside of the forest perimeter. There was always something to do, always panels to repair or replace, or illegal animal traps to destroy. It was an isolated job but it was a job non the less and it came with free accommodation for himself and his family which he just couldn't turn down, even if it did mean relocating to the middle of nowhere. Times were hard, and he knew he was lucky enough to get the job and it was nice that his two daughters were able to fully benefit from the wonders of nature that was all around them.

After making his way through the tough undergrowth and various hidden dips that the forest threw at him, he finally caught sight of the wooden lodge. Smoke danced up from the chimney and formed ghoulish patterns against the fading hew of the setting sun.

He was glad to be finally home, glad to see his family.

It had been a long day, and he was looking forward to finally getting some rest.

Henry opened the door that led into the entrance to the modest kitchen area; his wife was busy stirring a big pot of stew over by the stove. Heat filled the air and it was a nice contrast from the cooling evening that was lying down for the night outside. Emily and Hyacinth were sat by the fireside reading from the good book, something that Henry and Georgette made sure that they did religiously.

"Hello father" came the girlish voice of Emily as she peered up from where she sat. The glow of the fire silhouetted her outline in the background giving her an almost angelic look.

Georgette glanced over at her husband, he looked tired and weary, but she would never say that to him, she knew how hard he worked, and she was blessed for having such a good family.

"Henry, your home my love."

Georgette signalled to Emily to come and stir the pot of food while she went over and hugged her husband. Henry was thankful for the loving embrace and returned it with ease.

"Come here children, give your father a hug."

Although Henry was quite a stern man and set in his ways, he did love his family and more often than not couldn't resist the temptation in letting them know just how much he was glad to see them when he got home. Georgette kissed him on the cheek and instructed him to go wash for supper, as it was almost ready to be dished up.

After having a second helping to his wives flavoursome rabbit stew, Henry sat with his two daughters by the fire.

"Father can you please tell us one of your stories?" came the request from his youngest. Henry glanced down and gazed into the deep brown hazel eyes of Hyacinth, and although he was very tired, he would never refuse a story to his children.

"OK" he said, "but just a short one as time is getting on and I need to rest."

Both Emily and Hyacinth shifted their position and sat more comfortably and listened with open ears as their father began telling them the tale of the pirates and the hidden treasure. After Henry had finished telling his story he instructed his daughters to get ready for sleep, Henry was more than ready for his bed and judging by the myriad of yawns coming from his youngest daughter so was she. Emily and Hyacinth both kissed their parents goodnight and made their way up the ladder to their beds. Georgette made sure that they said their prayers and that they thanked the Lord for blessing them with such a loving father. It wasn't long before both girls were sound asleep.

Henry turned to Georgette and gave her a kiss on the forehead.

"I do love you" he said to her, Georgette smiled at him with her big beautiful forty year old eyes and nestled her head onto his chest. "Come on," Henry said, "let's get some shut-eye, this day has finally beaten me."

Georgette released her grip on her husband and set about getting herself ready for sleep, while Henry was shifting the burnt wood in the fire so that it was safe enough to leave for the night. Embers cracked and glowed as the last of the flames died down leaving just the orange glow from within its captive embrace. It wasn't long before the cabin lay silent, and the only noise that broke the eeriness was that of a faint low-pitched murmur coming from the lips of a dreaming eleven year old.

Henry awoke to the screeching of his wife Georgette.

Thick black smoke billowed across the entirety of the cabin making it almost impossible to see or breath. Flames, as red as the burning sun danced all around them and the only thing Henry could think of was his daughters.

He had to act fast.

Georgette was screaming and cowering on the bed with the blanket pulled up to her chin, tears streamed from her eyes and the look of sheer horror on her face was set in stone as she realised exactly what was happening to them. Henry could hear the shouts and screams coming from across the other side of the burning lodge.

"Mother, Father please help us."

Emily and Hyacinth were trapped as the flames licked the bottom of their bed. Henry, by now in a state of panic, jumped up from the bed, heat blasted him in the face, scorching his hair in the process, the smell of burnt hair made him gag, he had to get to his daughters. All around them the heavyset timbers of the wooden lodge creaked and moaned under the pressure of the rabid flames.

Henry tried in vain to reach his daughters but was beaten back time after time by the angry flames. There was no way to reach them. All

Henry could do now was to plead with God to save them, a plea that went unheard.

Henry turned to face his wife, sheer desperation had become of them as flames crept out from every side and every wall, and it was then he concluded that there was no way out for any of them, they were all going to perish in this inferno.

The sound of breaking timbers erupted as Henry turned just in time to see one of his daughters - he couldn't tell which one - fall from the ledge where their bed was, flames melting her skin as she fell silently and hit the ground with a sickening thump. Her body, now a mass of melted skin and blackened extremities, cracked and bubbled under the extreme heat of the raging fire.

Henry felt numb; it was as if everything fell silent.

The main beam of the timber roof began to buckle and split, splinters of burning wood rained down on him before finally giving way to the intense heat. The beam split across the middle and came toppling down on top of him. Georgette screamed as burning timbers pinned her to the side of the cabin.

Henry gazed over at his wife, who was now lying motionless and on fire, he whispered the words '*I love you*' as the rest of the timber roof collapsed and engulfed the family in a shroud of hellish fire.

One

Jonathan Matthews held the unopened envelope in his hand, he had been waiting for this to come all week, and he was hoping and praying that it was the good news he had been waiting on.

"Well go on, open it then, don't keep us in suspense any longer." Jonathan looked over at his wife Lisa, she looked even more nervous than he did, which was understandable given the fact that he would be uprooting the whole family into the middle of nowhere if the news was good.

"Ok, here goes" he said.

Jonathan looked down one last time at the brown envelope in his hand. He studied the bold black ink address on the top of it, *The Eden Forestry Project*, the words jumped out at him. Jonathan closed his eyes and took a deep breath, before sliding his finger inside the lip of the envelope and tearing it open.

Lisa waited for him to fully read what the letter said and after a couple of minutes Jonathan turned to his wife, smiled and said

"I got it, I got the job, it's mine."

Lisa ran towards her husband and threw her arms around him. "Oh! Well done my love, I knew that you could do it."

Jonathan handed Lisa the letter for her to read, and to double check that he wasn't just imagining it. Lisa sat down on the couch and began to read what the letter had said.

*"**Dear Mr Matthews,***
I would like to thank you for your interest in the position of Forest Manager with our company Eden Projects.
As you can understand this position was highly sought after, and we have been inundated with applications - which has made this process particularly difficult, given the amount of possible candidates we had to interview.
I would like to thank you for your patience during the course of this process and as you are aware it was a hard decision to make, therefore I would like to take this opportunity to offer you the position of Forest Manager with our company.
Your recommendations and references all were of the highest standard and your previous employer - Cane Woods Forest Management - had nothing but praise and thanks for you.
I look forward to meeting with you again in due course, and I am sure that your time with Eden Projects Forest Management will be a pleasant one.
You are also aware that this position comes with its own accommodation, which consists of a three bedroomed lodge set in the heart of the forest itself.
I have enclosed the telephone number of my secretary who will be more than happy to help with any queries that you may have regarding this position.
Also, please find enclosed the particulars of the position, the job description and what is expected of you.
I will endeavour to meet with you in the coming weeks with a view to having you start in a month or so. Once again congratulations Mr Matthews
Sincerely yours
Edwin Malachi,
Head of Project Management

Lisa stood up from the couch, the smile plastered all over her face told a million stories.

"Oh, Jonathan, this is the break that we have been waiting for. These past six months have been tough on all of us, especially the girls."

Jonathan held his wife and kissed the top of her head.

"I know it's been hard since I was made redundant, and I know we had to tighten our belts, but hopefully this is the new beginning we have been waiting for."

Lisa glanced over to the table; a pile of unpaid bills was stacking up which had been causing the both of them endless sleepless nights.

"Finally, we can get back on track", she said.

Jonathan looked his wife in the eye,

"Are you sure this is the right decision for us, I mean we will be in the middle of nowhere, their won't be a hell of a lot for you to do there."

"Are you kidding me?" came Lisa's sharp reply, "I will be busier than ever, I will have the girls to home school plus look after the lodge and do all the daily chores that come with it."

Jonathan sighed, "that's not what I meant, what I mean to say is,"

Before Jonathan had a chance to finish the sentence Lisa planted her lips onto his and kissed him.

"Jonathan Matthews, I will have none of that you hear me." Jonathan smiled and nodded.

"We will have to sit the girls down tonight and give them the good news, although I am not quite sure how they will take it. After all we are taking them away from their friends and their schooling and going to the middle of nowhere."

"Shush now" Lisa said, "the girls will be fine, we will be in the middle of nature, what more can two young girls want? You know how Sandra is with nature, she maybe only ten years old, but she loves the outdoors, and as for Kimmie, well she looks after her younger sister. Anywhere she goes you know Sandra is not far behind."

Jonathan agreed with Lisa, "it's just nerves I guess as its no doubt the biggest decision we have ever had to make as a family, that and of course whether or not to eat your meatloaf."

Lisa gasped and playfully slapped her husband on the shoulder,

"Don't you be dissing my famous meatloaf!"

The two of them giggled like a pair of loved up teenagers before holding each other again.

"I love you Jonathan", Lisa said, once again he kissed her on the top of the head and whispered '*I love you*' back to his wife.

Two

The following few weeks were chaotic. Extremely chaotic!

Their rented house in the middle of the city was a messy 'cardboard-metropolis'. Piles of flat-packed cardboard boxes filled the spare bedroom and the dining room in anticipation of being filled with all the accumulated goods of the Matthews family, prior to their big move from their current home in an urban sprawl, into the middle of nowhere.

Sandra and Kimmie had both thrown tantrums.

'Why should we leave our school?'

'We can't leave our friends?'

'You both hate us and are taking us away, we don't want to go to live in the woods!!'

The girls had moaned and complained on a daily basis over the short time they'd known that they were leaving everything they knew. It was hard for the children, it was also difficult for Lisa; she would be on a huge learning curve when she took up the '*home schooling*' of their girls. She had been to college after she had finished high school and had trained as a teacher, so it wasn't a huge leap for her, but taking the future education of her two girls solely in her hands was. The lack of a supervisor or head teachers to go to when she felt that she needed some help really worried her. But get on with it she would and she'd make Jonathan proud of her in the process.

Being unemployed, Jonathan had time on his hands.

He had thrown himself into looking into his future career more and more. He was spending most of his waking hours reading up about the Eden Forestry Project and seeing where his new position would take him.

Having worked in a lower managerial post with Cane Woods, it was a step up the ladder as a job and the fact that it was actually a 'live in' position made it an even more enviable appointment when it was advertised, but to actually be successful at the interview was a dream come true.

Jonathan had thought how jealous the other interviewees must have felt when they found out that they were unsuccessful and that he had come out on top – but it was a time to learn, not to dwell on the past or current victories and learn he had.

Spending hours researching the position and the company prior to his interview had paid off and now the only way was forward.

In between reading up on the Eden Forestry Project, building the flat packed boxes and packing their belongings into the final product, Jonathan had spent a lot of time reassuring Lisa and the girls that everything would be ok and that this would be a 'new adventure' for their family.

"We'll have the most amazing times at our new house" he had told Lisa and the girls over supper. "We will look back on these days and wish that we had done this earlier."

"I just hope that you're right" Lisa had replied, pushing the peas around her plate in a clockwise motion with her fork – she didn't feel hungry at the moment, just stressed due to the move.

"Of course I'm right! When have I ever been wrong?"

Lisa stared at Jonathan, why was he always right? Well nearly always. There was the time that he had bought a car off a guy in the nearby O'Hannigans bar and was later woken that night by the local Sherriff, who had spotted the car on the Matthews drive and realised that it was a vehicle that had been reported stolen the day before. They had laughed at how stupid he'd been, until their sides ached from guffawing so much, but he stopped when he realised that he wouldn't be getting the money back. That was the only wrong thing he'd done since they had been together, which must have been a pretty good record, Lisa made mistakes all the time.

Looking at her husband across the table Lisa mouthed the words '*I want you*' as she tousled her hair, continually shovelling the peas past the steak, through the ketchup and around the fries, the fork making scratching noises as it dragged across the plate.

"I want a horse."

Lisa snapped out of her daydream and looked across at Kimmie, who had spoken her request out loud.

"If we are moving out to the country, I want to have my own horse and I shall call it Starfire," she said, looking between her mother and father, with the sweetest innocent smile on her twelve year old lips.

"And if Kimmie can have a horse, then I want a dog and I shall call it Skipper" replied Sandra, determined not to be left out. "And I shall look after him, but won't pick up the poo, as that will be daddy's job."

Everyone around the table laughed as they looked at Sandra. She was growing up to be just like her mother - headstrong, determined and no-nonsense. It wouldn't be long before she would be bossing her older sister around and taking control of all the playing situations.

"Well if you're both good girls and help you mommy with the move, I'm sure we can sort out some kind of deal, but we'll need to be careful of Rex as well," he commented, looking across at the jet-black cat that was curled up on the sofa, as he ran his fingers through his jet-black hair. Though he still thought of his hair as dark, he had noticed that small flecks of grey had appeared at either side of his head around his ears, when he was looking at his reflection in the mirror that morning.

'*Either I'm getting old or it's the stress of this move*' he'd thought to himself as he had finished his morning shave, wiping the excess foam on his neck off with a hand towel.

But he still had it and Lisa was proving that she still wanted a part of it, as she continued to stare as him from across the dinner table, running her fingers through her deep red locks. Growing up as a child, she had been bullied at school for having 'ginger' hair, but as she had got older, her hair had become her crowing glory and it was this and her voluptuous figure that had attracted her to Jonathan in the first place.

"I think it's time to get ready for bed now girls" said Lisa as she picked up the plates from the table and walking to the kitchen, tipped the remnants of the meals from the plates into the flip-top bin.

"When we get Skipper, I shall feed him my leftovers" announced Sandra from her seat, "and he shall be ever so grateful and sleep at the foot of my bed - until it is time for daddy to take him out for a poo!"

Everyone at the table - and Lisa in the kitchen - all laughed once more, apart from Sandra, who was sat up straight at the table looking very proud of herself. "And I will train Skipper to bark at any burglars and ghosties, so that we are safe in our new house."

"It'll be fine," said Jonathan, being very proud of his girls and what they were growing up to be. "Time for bed now, up the stairs and into your PJ's, mom will come up and tuck you up in five minutes.

With a scraping of chairs and gentle thuds of their tiny feet on the floor, Kimmie and Sandra headed up to their room.

"We haven't even told them yet, that they'll have a room each at the new house, have we? They'll be so pleased."

Looking at his wife Jonathan replied, "there'll be no more arguments about not enough room to play or that one of them was talking in their sleep or that the other one was snoring. It'll be total bliss."

And with that Jonathan took his wife by the hand and turning out the lights, led her upstairs to their bedroom.

As he undressed and got into bed, Lisa went into the girls' room and made sure that they were both tucked up and ready to go to sleep. When she had kissed them both goodnight and turned out the light, she walked across the hallway and into hers and Jonathan's bedroom.

"You know that we'll need to be quiet," she whispered as she slithered across the floor like a slippery sexual snake stalking her prey and dropping her clothes as she headed towards the bed.

"I know, I'll try my very best," he whispered between clenched teeth - his backache was back and with a vengeance; he thought that it was the bending over constantly all day, putting the boxes together, nothing more serious than that and just getting slightly older of course.

For the next hour, the thoughts of the move, the new job and their new forest dwelling were the furthest things from their mind. They both pleasured and pleased each other like never before, the thoughts of all debt problems and employment worries had floated away, giving them both a new lease of life and as they both climaxed, they heard one of their girls crying from the other room. Grabbing her dressing gown and brushing her hair from her eyes, Lisa headed the short few steps to the girl's bedroom.

Lisa found Sandra sobbing in the lower bunk bed, Kimmie sound asleep up above.

"I really want a doggie mommy" she blubbered, as her mom put her arm around her shoulders.

"We'll see what we can do if you're a good girl," said Lisa, laying Kimmie down and tucking her in.

"I'll be really good, you'll see," she said as she started to drift off immediately, snores already emanating from her as Lisa walked out of the door and back to Jonathan.

Getting back into bed, she realised that he was already asleep and snuggled into the back of him, spooning him to within an inch of his life, but he didn't notice, the snores already filling her head like a low rumble of distant thunder on a stormy winters night. She needed to get some sleep too as the move was only a few days away and they had so much still to do, and with that she drifted off as well, dreaming of mountains of cardboard boxes and a dog called Skipper sat astride them…

Three

The next few days flew by in a flurry of wrapping paper, boxes and tape and then it was the day of the big move.

The removal truck arrived at the Matthews apartment block at just a little after 8am on the day that they were due to set off on their new adventure.

The majority of the families possessions were already boxed up in the rooms, with their 'room destination' in the new house marked clearly on the top in marker pen. Large black capital letters stated 'KITCHEN', 'BATHROOM', 'and DAD'S MAN CAVE' amongst the five dozen large boxes, carrying all their worldly possessions to a new life in the countryside.

Rex the cat was already packaged up in his cat basket on the kitchen counter and the girls were finishing their cereal at the breakfast bar.

"Mom, can we still eat Fruit Loops in our new home?" asked Kimmie, as she scooped another spoonful of brightly coloured cereal into her mouth.

"Of course pudding, why not?" replied Lisa as she carried on unplugging the electrical items, putting the kettle, the toaster and the waffle iron into another box, ceiling it with tape and writing 'KITCHEN' on the top.

"Can I have chocolate for breakfast when we move in?" queried Sandra looking at her mother over the counter.

"No you cannot" she replied. "Nothing will change that much, rules are still rules" she smiled as she leant over and tousled her daughters hair in a rough, but playful, way.

"Which room do you want us to clear first?"

Lisa turned around to see a large man in green overalls - named Brad, as it stated on his patch - standing in her doorway scratching his head. He reminded Lisa of her Uncle Bob - always in overalls, head under the hood of his car, hands covered in oil and dust.

"If you could start on the bedrooms and work your way along the hall" she replied, a little unnerved at the 'creepy' way that he was staring at her girls. She felt a shiver go down her spine, it almost felt like a premonition or just a generally bad feeling about the move – which was a shame as she was really looking forward to their new life.

In their bedroom Jonathan was taping shut the final boxes containing his books and paperwork for the new job. He was going to miss the place. He'd lived in Boston, Massachusetts, for most of his life, apart from when he'd gone away to New York for University and now he was going to leave the big city behind and move to the Manuel F. Correllus State Forest on Martha's Vineyard, a small section of which was managed by the Eden Forestry Project and not the Department of Conservation and Recreation.

"I'm going to miss you most," he said looking out the window at his view across the city – the hustle and bustle of Boston in the early morning always made him feel ready for the day and the view of the cars piling down the streets in the autumn – as the leaves fell – constantly made him feel like he was at home.

"What time do we need to catch the ferry?" Lisa called from the kitchen.

"There's a ferry at 2:45pm that we can catch from the Steamship Authority and it leaves from Wood's Hole. Should only take about an hour or so to get across, especially as there's no wind today, the crossing will be calm."

Over the next hour all the boxes were taken down to the removal truck by the three strong crew and the Matthews family locked up the property, posting the keys in through the letterbox and took their own personal items – and Rex the cat – down to their station wagon and packed it all in the back. The girls climbed in and Jonathan and Lisa got into the front, he starting the car and pulling out after the already steadily moving truck with all their worldly goods in transit.

****

It took two hours and forty-five minutes to drive from Boston to Wood's Hole, which was good time keeping as the roads were fairly steady flowing from when they left.

Wood's Hole was a small area in the town of Falmouth and the Steamship Authority (or SSA) was the car ferry to Martha's Vineyard which left from there on a regular basis; it was the only car ferry to the island and so tended to be very busy in the summer, but now being autumn it was only half full.

As they followed the removal truck onto the ferry, they settled in for their 45-minute journey to their destination and their new peaceful life away from the chaotic city.

When the ferry pulled in to the wharf at Vineyard Haven, Jonathan and Lisa were both amazed at how pleasant and quiet the town seemed to be.

With a population of just over 2000 inhabitants – but many more in the summer months – Vineyard Haven was one of three populated areas on the island, the others being Edgartown and Oak Bluffs – both having double the population of where they had just arrived. Edgartown was an old whaling port and Oak Bluffs was the original home of the American Indian tribe, the Wampanoag, who had been decimated in the 17th century by a plague.

Vineyard Haven was a picture postcard of a town, with many wooden white fronted buildings, from stores and bars to the population's homes. The area had originally been known as '*Nobnocket*' by the Wampanoag, but that name had faded away into history as the town's population had grown and the tribe's population had decreased.

As they slowly followed the removal truck inland, there were gradually less and less homes at the side of the road and when they finally took a right turn and up a dirt track towards their new house, they were truly on their own.

"Are we there yet?" came the usual comment from Sandra as they headed further up the rough and bumpy track to their destination.

"My tummy is rumbling, what time is dinner?" asked Kimmie. Of the girls she was the one who always enjoyed a good meal everyday, whereas Sandra could take it our leave it where mealtimes were concerned.

As they drove up the track Jonathan rubbed at his chin – was he really going to enjoy being out here in the middle of nowhere, with mainly just his family for company? He coughed clearing his throat and trying desperately to calm his nerves and feel positive about his new position.

At the same time as Jonathan was wondering about the way forward, Lisa was having her own thoughts. Was it going to be a big mistake or the making of them as a family? How was she going to be able to cope with the home schooling of two fairly boisterous young girls and whom could she go to for help when it was needed? She scratched at a stain on her jeans as she kept her concentration on the way ahead, trying like Jonathan to remain optimistic about their family move.

Moving through a clearing in the trees, the area opened up and in front of them stood their new dwelling, at the far end of track – the end of the line. Standing tall and proud at the end of the path, their new family home was what was known as a '*Greek Revival House*' which were in abundance in Edgartown and had a large front porch area and columns either side of the front door. These houses were quite historically formal and were popular with the captains of the whaling boats and were also used by the shipbuilders, but for one to be here, in the middle of the woods, made it stand out ever further and seem more eloquent than ever.

The truck had pulled up at the front of the property and Jonathan pulled into the left of it, giving the 'movers' enough room for them to both get out of their van and manoeuvre their way past the two vehicles and up the steps into the property.

Walking up the sturdy wooden steps to the front door of their new property, Jonathan delved into his pocket for the keys and found that they weren't there.

'Shit' he thought to himself, had he left the keys in Boston? He couldn't have, he'd picked them up and…

"They're in my shoulder bag" he said out loud, making Lisa turn around from her viewing of their new home and the grounds around them.

"What are?"

"Oh nothing, just reminding myself where the house keys are" he replied, as he walked back to the car with a sense of relief and picked up his shoulder bag. Unzipping the top he found the keys, in amongst his letters in reference to the job and the maps and guides to area of Martha's Vineyard.

Turning on his heel, Jonathan walked back towards the property, swinging the keys on his finger as he strode into the heart of his family's new life.

Sauntering up the steps with Lisa beside him, he slotted the keys into the lock and pushed the door open.

The house smelt a little 'musty' having been empty since the last Forest Manager had left, in what was rumoured to have been a hurry – though no one had really explained to Jonathan why or what had happened for him to suddenly vanish. Apparently he had said that there was something wrong with the position and that the woods '*just didn't seem to be, all they appeared to be*' – Jonathan had taken this as the previous manager having some kind of allergy and that the woods had brought it on to a more heightened level. He had locked up the property and posted the keys back to Edwin Malachi via secured USPS delivery.

Looking around the ground floor, the property was beautifully decorated and furnished; they had really fallen on their feet with this 'live in' position. From the leather sofas and chairs to the HD widescreen TV on the wall to the PS4, the property was kitted out with the best in furniture and modern technology.

As Lisa walked into the kitchen, she found that it was fully stocked with what appeared to be all new products – microwave, food mixer, waffle iron and more – she really could have left a lot of the items behind that she had brought with them.

As they walked around the ground floor the removal team came over the threshold and asked, "which rooms do you want us to bring the boxes up for first?" All three of them standing in the doorway looking like extras from 'The Shawshank Redemption' in their dirty overalls and sweaty faces.

"If you can do all of the downstairs first and then the bedrooms last," Lisa replied as she and Jonathan walked up the stairs to the check out the bedrooms and the bathroom.

A fifteen-minute tour of their home covered all bases and they then walked out to the car and the girls, squeezing past a sweaty man carrying a large box marked ‘KITCHEN’.

As they got out, the girls were standing on the edge of the property, near the trees – which marked the start of the Forest that Jonathan would be managing. They appeared to be deep in conversation with both themselves and someone that appeared to be out of sight in amongst the dense undergrowth, bushes and trees.

“C’mon girls, let’s go see your bedrooms,” Lisa called across the driveway and the grass area beyond that, which surrounded the house.

The girls turned to their mother and then turned back and said goodbye to whomever they had been speaking to and went running over to where Lisa was waiting for them.

“I think I’m really going to enjoy it here,” screeched Sandra.

“Me too,” agreed Kimmie as they both took their mothers hands and walked towards the house.

“Why do you think that then girls?”

“Because we’ve already made friends and we’ve only been here for fifteen minutes” answered Kimmie, all smiles and full of positivity.

“Who have you made friends with then?”

Sandra looked up at her mother and smiled “with the two sisters of course, Emily and Hyacinth”…

Four

Over the next few days, things in the house were somewhat hectic to say the least. Boxes, piled up on top of one another, but the boxes were slowly but surely getting emptied and their contents finding their way to a more permanent place, and the rooms were finally starting to look liveable. The girls seemed to have settled in quite nicely with little or no arguing amongst themselves. Lisa had noticed that the children kept on making reference to the girls, it puzzled her at the start but Lisa didn't put any notice onto it as she had far too much to concern herself with than her children's imaginary friends, besides she found it quite cute.

Over the next few weeks, things started to take shape, Jonathan was loving the job and managed to get in every night for around six o'clock - a nice time to have tea. Kimmie and Sandra had taken to the new house really well and were looking forward to their mother home teaching them.

On the Tuesday morning, Lisa had called the two girls to get up for breakfast. Today was the day she was going to start their lessons. They were already almost a month behind, but luckily for Lisa she was able to get access to the curriculum from the school so that she could at least follow on with some sort of plan. Sandra was the first to come down the stairs for breakfast, her hair was still messy and she still looked tired.

"Good morning sweet pea, how are you today? are you looking forward to starting your lessons?"

"Good morning mum, I'm tired, I didn't get much sleep last night, I kept on waking up"

"Oh why was that hun? you went to bed pretty early and when I checked in on the both of you, you were sound asleep"

"I don't know mum, I just kept on waking up",

"Well maybe you were over tired and your brain was finding it hard to switch off!"

"Yeah I guess" Sandra replied.

"Where is your sister, I want to get a start on your lessons sharpish, we have a lot to do today"

Lisa walked into the hallway and shouted up the stairs for Kimmie to get a move on, but Lisa got no reply back. Lisa sighed and made her way up the winding staircase towards the top floor. She could hear talking coming from Kimmie's bedroom, so she knew that she was awake. As Lisa reached the last step, Kimmie appeared from her bedroom, her big beaming smile was enough to melt the ice caps.

"Oh there you are, I have been calling you, did you not hear me?"

"Sorry mum no, I was chatting with Hyacinth, she is a little sad today"

Lisa looked at her eldest daughter with a baffled look on her face.

"And who may I ask is Hyacinth?"

Kimmie turned her head to look at the floor; she became shy and secretive, which was not in her nature at all.

"She is one of my friends, mom, it's her birthday today"

Lisa stared at her daughter before going over and giving her a hug.

"Well happy birthday to you Hyacinth, but I need to borrow my daughter for the day".

"It's ok mom, she said that she likes you"

"Oh does she now, well you just tell Miss Hyacinth I'm very grateful, now come on you, get down stairs for breakfast, we have a lot to get through today".

Kimmie smiled at Lisa and made her way downstairs. Lisa stood and watched as her daughter descended the stairs humming the tune to Black Beauty. Lisa was so proud of her daughters. Something moved at the corner of her eye startling her back to reality. A shadow seemed to have moved across the doorway to Kimmie's bedroom. Lisa walked towards the half opened doorway and then suddenly stopped in her tracks. An ice-cold chill snaked its way down her spine causing her to shiver. She pushed open the door to the bedroom and it was as it should be. Nothing out of place, and all normal. Lisa shook her head and laughed to herself, *'you old fool Lisa, you're going mad in your old age'*. She shrugged the cold feeling off and closed the door behind her.

Five

Jonathan had been walking for miles, or so it seemed to him. The sun was beating down hard on his forehead and sweat dripped off the bottom of his chin.

He decided to take a break from the searing heat under a huge oak tree; its branches sprawled out from all directions offering him some good shading. The Correlus Woods in which he now spent most of his time in were overpowering. It would have been so easy to get lost out here had he not studied the pathways and 'cut-throughs' religiously on the map that had been provided for him. He rested for a bit, basking in the cooling shade of the trees. Reaching into his rucksack, he took a long swig of the now lukewarm bottle of lemonade that Lisa had made for him. Jonathan was loving the peacefulness, but more importantly he was getting a sense of pride back now that he was working again.

After a short rest, Jonathan composed himself once more. He had to go and check on the outer perimeter fence. It was easy access for poachers and illegal hunters hoping to bag themselves a buck or two. As he started to walk down the far right mud trail that led him out towards the edge of the forest, he came across an opening in the trees. The clearing opened up to around twenty feet or so, and was lined with greenery on all sides. The ground itself looked like it had been disturbed at some point in time as the soil itself was darker in patches.

'*I wonder what on earth was here*', he shrugged his shoulders and dismissed it before carrying on his hike.

Deep within the soil, the rusted bones of the van slowly corroded into the depths of the earth. A silent unspoken grave.

After finally reaching the edge of the forest, Jonathan threw his rucksack down in the gorse. The perimeter fence stretched as far as his eyes could see before reaching a bend and disappearing around to the left. Jonathan inspected the fence for any breakages or weak spots, and hunted around for any signs of human activity. To his relief the fence looked as if it were intact and the forest itself was void of any human interference, apart from his own.

Jonathan spent a good hour inspecting the various weak points and potential areas of concern before calling it a day. He was tired, the sun was unforgiving and the day had gotten hotter.

"God damn Mosquitoes" as he vehemently swatted another insect off the side of his arm. He picked his bag up and turned to make his way back to the house, that is when he saw it, him, hell he wasn't sure himself. Over the far end of the trail Jonathan was sure he saw a man standing watching him. An older looking man in a faded blue overall with a scruffy looking beard, he seemed to be grinning as the sun reflected off the yellow stains of his teeth. Jonathan had to look twice. But he was gone on the second glance.

"I think this sun is getting to me Jonathan old boy!" he said as he wiped the sweat from his face with the back of his hand. Time to go home.

Six

Within less than half an hour Jonathan rounded the bushes – the leaves hanging like burnt auburn bats, from the end of the nearly bare twigs - and headed up the path to his house.

It had been another hard, but enjoyable days work and if all the days were as good as today, he could see himself carrying on in this position for the foreseeable future; perhaps even until retirement loomed its pensionable head, but that was many years away still at the moment.

As he gradually neared the house he could see all the windows with their curtains wide open. In the downstairs window he could see Lisa, sat at the table in the lounge and in one of the upstairs bedroom windows, he noticed that Kimmie was standing staring out, oblivious to anything that was happening and not even noticing her father coming home from another busy day at work.

And then he noticed that she was talking, making quite animated movements with her head and waving her hands around for further emphasis on the points that she appeared to be explaining.

Her lips were moving and she was having some kind of conversation, as she laughed, nodded and shook her head at almost regular intervals. Then Jonathan noticed that there was a hand on her shoulder, a small child like hand.

'Must be Sandra' he thought to himself.

But then his whole world began to spin in turmoil as he noticed Sandra appear in the downstairs window with her mother, waving at her father, as she noticed him coming home for supper.

His eyes darted to the upstairs window and Kimmie was still standing there talking, but the hand on her shoulder was slowly moving towards the window and then throwing it wide open.

As Jonathan neared the front steps he saw the hand appear once more on Kimmie's shoulder and then her saw her whole body shoved forward, as she was pushed with some force out of the open window.

Then the world all slowed down for Jonathan.

"Noooooooooooooooooooooo" Jonathan screamed as his daughter soared in slow motion out of the open window and began her descent towards the garden below. Time then slowed down as Jonathan stared in utter shock, as his daughter fell from the first floor, passing the lounge window and hitting the grass and dirt to the right of the front door in a crumpled heap.

Lisa looked up and Sandra screamed as they saw Kimmie pass their window and land in the yard outside, heavily hitting the dirt with her left shoulder.

Dropping his bag, Jonathan ran the final few steps to the place where Kimmie was lying, crying in pain as she writhed on the ground. A small splinter of bone from her clavicle had torn through her t-shirt and was poking out like a bloody, pointing skeletal finger.

"Oh my god, try not to move" he called to his daughter, as Lisa and Sandra came out of the house, Sandra bursting into tears, sobbing as she saw her sister howling in pain on the ground.

"There, there, it'll all be fine" he said, pulling a handkerchief from his pocket to stem the blood flow, from the area around the bone that was still protruding through the material of her t-shirt.

Her once pretty white floral t-shirt, was quickly becoming stained as the blood seeped out of the wound and the fresh material rapidly soaked up the swiftly spreading maroon stain.

"Mummy, it hurts really bad" she blubbed in between deep breaths, as she tried to talk to her mother and father, not seeming to understand how she had ended up outside the house.

Lisa bit her lip as she hugged Sandra, trying not to make the situation any worse than it already was, as her husband worked on stemming the now constant flow.

"You'll be ok baby, Daddy will sort it all out and make you better" she said trying to calm both her daughters down, with some reassuring words.

As Jonathan worked on keeping Kimmie still he called over to Lisa.

"Phone the Vineyard Medical Centre and tell them we're on our way".

With that Jonathan carefully scooped her up in his arms and walked towards the station wagon, Lisa rapidly punching the numbers into her phone as she walked behind, Sandra - still snivelling - following closely behind her.

Eventually the call connected and Lisa put the phone to her ear and began to relay to the Medical Centre what had just happened at their property.

"Hello, my daughter has had an accident at our home" she said, when the phone was answered and went on to explain what had happened and the condition that her daughter was in now – clarifying that a shattered bone was already poking out through her skin and that she was bleeding fairly badly.

Lisa - looking worried - came off the phone and turned to Jonathan as he carefully put Kimmie into the back of their vehicle, helping Sandra into the car as well.

"Is she going to be ok?"

"Of course she is, we've just got to get her looked at ASAP," replied Jonathan as he opened the door for Lisa and walked hurriedly around to the driver's side of the vehicle, opening the door and sliding into his seat in one swift move, starting the engine and leaving their homestead in a rush.

Clicking the air con on, he drove as fast as he could, heading down the track to the main road, not noticing the small figure in the still open upstairs window, as she waved them goodbye as they began to make rapidly increasing distance between themselves and the house.

Then the mysterious little girl gradually began to fade into the background and with that she was gone; suddenly all the lights in the house lit up as the car went out of sight, the intensity of the brightness made the house look like a star – a white super nova - and then the lights, just like the little girl, faded away back to darkness and the house was quiet once more.

Seven

The short drive to the Medical Centre in Vineyard Haven was much quicker than they both expected - and remembered – and Jonathan put it down to driving as fast as he could, mostly in a blind panic. Lisa soothed both of the girls by constantly speaking and reassuring them that it would be much better soon.

As they pulled up at the kerb outside the Medical Centre, two nurses and an on call doctor – who were already aware of the their imminent arrival - rushed out and helped Lisa and Jonathan remove Kimmie from the car, taking her immediately by wheelchair in through the doors and into triage.

All the other people who were sitting in the waiting room with a variety of ailments, from bruised knuckles to extreme dental pain to broken fingers and migraines, took second place to Kimmie as she was taken through to be assessed by the medical team, as blood continued to drip from her wound – leaving a trail through the corridor of the Centre.

The nurses removed her t-shirt as Jonathan, Lisa and Sandra watched on, their arms all around each other, hugging and spreading the love, all praying that she would be ok – and soon.

"She's lost a lot of blood" one of the nurses commented as she dropped the red soaked rag of a t-shirt on the floor, whilst the doctor looked at the protruding bone and the severity of the situation.

"It's a nasty break that's for sure; there's nothing for it, she's going to have to go to the mainland," he said rubbing his chin as he debated the next move that they'd need to take.

"Ring Dale with the chopper, he's going to have to fly her and her family to the mainland for treatment – we're not designed to cope with something this severe at the Centre or at the hospital on the island. If we catch him now, she'll be airborne and on her way within the next ten minutes."

At the nurse station one of the staff phoned Dale the emergency helicopter pilot and true to the doctors word, the helicopter landed in the car park and all the family were on their way back to the mainland in just short of eight minutes.

The flight was quick, the weather was calm and the sea far below was deathly still and within only twenty minutes the helicopter landed on the mainland and a waiting ambulance took them straight to the nearby General Hospital.

As they went in through the swinging doors to the Casualty Department, Jonathan and Lisa looked at each other and forced a smile – especially for the girls – it was going to be a long night.

****

Back at the Matthews home, all was silent.

The only noises that were breaking the hush were the crickets in the field to the left of the property and even they seemed to be making less noise that usual, almost as if they were afraid to be blamed for anything that was taking place.

It was dark now and the house was in totally darkness as well.

Then all things began to change…

At first a dull glow began to emanate from the upstairs window, which was still wide open from when Kimmie had fallen out of it. Starting off as a burnt amber colour, as the intensity grew, the glow changed gradually into a brighter red, then orange, developing into yellow and then eventually an incredibly powerful white light.

As the light became brighter, the room lit up like it was in a spotlight and the small girl walked towards the open space, stretching out her arms to close the windows. Not even touching them with her hands, they closed back into the frame and hands passed through the glass as they moved.

In the radiating light her arms and hands glistened like the scales of a fish. The child's arms were scaly and burnt, looking like someone who had been in an accident, with her skin only just beginning to heal.

Then the dazzling light began to fade, as slowly as it had brightened the area, the room was once again plunged into darkness and the little girl faded gently back into her surroundings and she was gone.

With the house all closed up once more, the area was at peace again. The noise of the crickets from the field next to the house began to intensify and the wind began to pick up. All seemed to be back to normal and the house seemed to be waiting the return of the Matthews family.

Rex the cat was wondering around the outside of the house, keeping a safe distance from the steps, as if he was being extremely cautious about going any closer.

Then suddenly Rex's back arched, as if he sensed something.

First he started hissing and then he spun around, as the man in the pale blue overall moved carefully towards the house from the field beside the property. His scruffy beard still looked unkempt and the sun was catching the reflections of the sky on his badly conditioned moist teeth.

As he approached the steps at the front of the house, he almost appeared to float up them and then on approaching the front door, he leaned forward and slowly 'faded' through the entrance and disappeared inside the property.

The Matthews home had a 'new guest' and Rex hissed at the door in an act of defiance. Cats have been known to sense things and Rex was detecting an aura of foreboding as he leant against the base of the steps and licked his paws, before turning and heading away towards the open fields.

Eight

Kimmie awoke from her operation later that night. She was still groggy from the anaesthetic and found it uncomfortable with her arm all bandaged up. She turned to see her father and mother waiting by her bedside smiling back at her.

"Hello my princess", Jonathan said, "How are you feeling?"

Kimmie groaned and tried to position herself to a better position with little joy.

"I'm ok daddy, it just hurts a little".

Kimmie's mom was stroking the top of her head; she had a tear in her eye and a concerned look upon her face.

"You gave us one hell of a fright darling, do you remember what happened," Lisa said.

Kimmie averted her eyes to look straight at the ceiling; the glow off the light above her bed hurt her eyes a little.

"No mom, I just sort of fell I think?"

Jonathan remembered what he thought he had seen earlier that day, but was reluctant to push his daughter for answers at that moment.

Jonathan left his daughters cubicle to go and use the bathroom, Lisa sat patiently by her daughter's side, while Sandra was busy colouring in one of her books on the floor by the foot of the bed. The door opened and doctor Monroe, one of the main doctors who was taking care of Sandra came in to see Jonathan and Lisa.

"My husband has just popped to the lavatory" Lisa said, he won't be long.

"Mrs Matthews, may I see you outside for a moment please".

Lisa kissed her daughter on the forehead and told Kimmie she would be just outside,

"Sandra is here with you".

Lisa left the room and Kimmie could see her dad through the gap in the frosted window, as he came back, and they both stood talking to the doctor.

Sandra stood up and walked over to her sister. She didn't seem that bothered that her older sister was in hospital, but she was still young and didn't quite know exactly what was going on. Sandra leaned forward and whispered into Kimmie's ear.

"Hyacinth says she is sorry, she tried to grab you as you went forward but was unable to stop you, She says it was a bad man".

Kimmie stared at her sister; she didn't remember much of what had happened up until then. Then without warning, a flash, an image, a feeling crept up from inside her. She remembered suddenly feeling icy cold, before plummeting forward through the opened window. Kimmie turned her head again and said,

"No, I slipped and if mom and dad ask anything that's what happened ok".

Sandra looked at her sister and smiled,

"Okely dokely" she said before returning back to the floor to continue on with her colouring.

****

Kimmie spent the next week in the hospital and she was more than glad when she was discharged. There was only so much of being cooped up in a hospital bed she could take. Jonathan arrived at the hospital to pick her up while Lisa stayed at home with Sandra to prepare lunch for when they both got back. Kimmie smiled when she saw her dad coming up the hallway.

"Are you all ready kiddo?" Jonathan said in a light-hearted voice. "I sure am dad, I can't wait to go home".

Jonathan and Kimmie both said thank you to the doctors and nurses that had taken care of her and left the hospital for home.

The journey home took longer than expected as the traffic from the mainland was at a crawling pace due to the new roadworks that had gone up a few days earlier.

"What do you recon kiddo, if I put my head out the window and do an ambulance siren, do you think they would move for us?"

Jonathan laughed as he looked at his daughter. Kimmie smiled back at him, the innocence in her face was pure and Jonathan felt a warm sensation from within that only a father could have for his daughter.

"I don't know dad, you could try but I don't expect it would work somehow."

Eventually the old station wagon crept up through the roadworks and was clear of the build up of traffic.

"Thank God for that" Jonathan said.

It was another good hour until they arrived back at their home.

Nine

Things remained reasonably quiet over the next few weeks, and both girls got stuck into their homework that Lisa had printed off for them. The home schooling was going pretty well for them and Lisa was impressed at how her girls had adapted.

On Tuesday, Lisa had set aside some time to do cooking with the girls. After carefully measuring out all the ingredients and cutting up fresh chicken that Jonathan had picked up, she placed them in the fridge for when they were ready. The girls loved cooking and Lisa loved spending time with them, other than doing other subjects like maths, or English. Sandra and Kimmie had finished the written test on algebra that Lisa had printed off that morning, and handed them to their mom. Lisa was impressed with their attitude. They were both looking forward to their cooking lesson.

"Right girls, shall we do some cooking,"

Lisa smiled at her daughters as they hurried down the stairs to the kitchen. Both girls put their aprons on and washed their hands.

"Kimmie can you please get the ingredients from the fridge please, and put them on the table".

Kimmie did as her mother asked and went to the fridge. Lisa was standing at the stove putting a pan of water on when suddenly she was startled by a horrendous scream coming from Kimmie. Lisa turned towards her. Kimmie was hiding behind the table and pointing over to the fridge.

"Sandra what's happened to your sister?"

"I don't know mom, she just screamed."

Kimmie was in tears and was shaking. Lisa hurried over to the fridge and opened it. To her horror and disgust, huge flies darted out from the shelves, and the freshly cut chicken was alive with thick grey coloured maggots which were falling off the plate.

"Oh Christ that's disgusting" she said.

Lisa quickly grabbed a small towel and covered the rotting chicken.

"Quick Sandra open the back door, I will put them in the outside bin."

Sandra quickly opened the door and Lisa ran out. Maggots dropped to the kitchen floor and slowly poked and prodded their bodies towards the stench that was lingering in the air. Sandra stepped on them. Their tiny bodies popped under the weight of her trainer and little blobs of thick creamy pus squirted out onto the kitchen floor.

Lisa came back in. The smell of rotting chicken was heavy to the nostrils. After Lisa had finished washing the fridge and mopping the floors after the maggot incident, she sat down at the table. The girls had gone upstairs to play to keep out of her way as she cleaned. Lisa couldn't fathom what or how it could have happened. The chicken was fresh from the store and smelled totally fine when she prepared it. A buzzing noise came from the blinds of the kitchen window. As she looked across, one thick black bodied fly hovered frantically at the glass.

Lisa rolled up the pages of her copy of the teaching times and squashed the insect. The feeling of disgust made her skin crawl.

"Dirty horrible things" she said as she threw the magazine in the bin. She still couldn't make any sense of what had occurred earlier.

****

Later on that night when her husband came home, Lisa explained to him why they were only having a light supper of salad and a tin of ham. Jonathan was fine with it as he was tired from a hard day's slog. He too couldn't make much sense of it and put it down to having some dodgy meat.

"I wouldn't read too much into it," he said to Lisa, "chicken goes off pretty quick in this heat".

It was getting late and Lisa got the girls into bed.

"We will try again when I get some fresh ingredients," she said to Kimmie. "How are you feeling?"

"I'm ok mom, I am pretty sleepy".

Lisa tucked her into bed, kissed her on the forehead and turned off her light.

****

He stood watching, waiting from beyond the realm of reality.

A hunger that lusted into every part of his sick mind. The innocence and frailty of her immaturity stoked a fire deep within him. He had the control; he possessed the power this time.

With his dirty faded blue overalls and oil stained hands, he easily went from one room to the next. They slept soundly as his evil grew stronger and stronger.

Sandra stirred in her sleep, restless as the air within her room became thick, clammy, making it difficult to breath.

As she opened her eyes to the darkness, she thought she could see a figure, an uninvited guest lurking at the bottom of her bed. But as she sat up and waited for her eyes to adjust to the dim glow of the crescent moon, all remained the same.

Ten

"Mommie, can I sleep in with you tonight?" asked Sandra, "I'm just not sleeping 'properly' in my room," she continued, curling her hair around her finger as she spoke, tugging at the strands when her mother failed to respond straightaway.

Lisa was at the sink – as she was most mornings – cleaning the remainder of the dishes from breakfast. Jonathan had already left for work several hours earlier and the girls were both in the kitchen at the table, waiting to start that days 'schooling'.

"What do you mean by that?" Lisa replied looking up from the washing up bowl - full of dishes - her hands covered in soapy suds.

"Every time I try to go to sleep, I keep seeing things in my room, a man at the bottom of my bed"

Lisa turned around and looked at her girls. They were certainly both growing up, but it wasn't like her younger daughter to be frightened at night; sometimes Kimmie would have nightmares and come in crying to her and Jonathan, but Sandra, even since her sisters accident, was the strongest and least scared of her two daughters – even though she was the youngest.

"Don't be silly, there's nothing bad in your room. If you want you can sleep in Kimmie's room with her for a few nights? We can put up the camp bed and your older sister can be in charge if you like?"

"OK" she replied and began writing the days date at the top of the page in her exercise book, ready for that days lessons.

Lisa wiped the suds of her hands on the apron that was hanging around her neck, took it off and hung it up to dry on the back of the kitchen door, as the water from the empty bowl in the sink, washed down the drain in a bubbly clockwise motion.

"Well ladies, todays lesson will be about poetry and rhyming. Now I know that both of you are already very good at this and that's why we'll have a little completion, with a prize at the end" said Lisa, smiling at her girls – she was already loving the home schooling and it was so far going like a dream. The girls were still extremely keen and she was enjoying the fact that they were happy to have their mother teaching them.

"What do we need to write a poem about?" asked Kimmie, taking the lead in the poetry lesson already.

"I want you both to write a poem about living here and your new life on Martha's Vineyard."

Lisa looked at the girls, who were both staring into space as they each looked for inspiration. Although they were both still very young, they had a wonderful grasp of the English language and reading and writing were both their favourite subjects. Math was a difficult subject for Sandra and her big sister struggled with it too, but they were still achieving good results and higher than that of the equivalent students of their age would be gaining in classrooms all across America. Science lessons were always a bit of a chore, but cookery and religious studies came quite easy to the girls as well. All in all, Lisa felt blessed with two girls that were keen to learn and produced a high quality of grades that any parent would be proud of. If they carried on as they were, Lisa could see them both going on to University in later years and gaining amazing results and qualifications, leading on to successful careers.

Kimmie seemed to be an ideal candidate – even at her age – for veterinary school; she loved animals so much and was missing Rex, who had already been absent for several days, but cats did tend to wander off for days on end at times.

Whereas on the other hand, Sandra was the more artistic of the girls and could paint pictures, which for a girl of her age, were very realistic and almost good enough to sell in the shops on the island. She was best at painting scenes of the beaches and the trees, but her very best detailed work was in the flowers that she continually painted when they had their weekly art lessons, on a Tuesday afternoon, just after lunch.

Lisa picked up that days local newspaper and read through the articles as the girls rubbed their heads, stared into space and stroked their hair as they began to write their poems.

Lisa flicked through the local news and noticed that even Kimmie had been reported for her accident – *'obviously a slow news day'* she thought to herself as she cut the piece out to show Jonathan when he came home from work.

As she carried on reading, the girls carried on writing and then writing some more, now in the full flows of poetic prose, the girls both scribbled away in their notebooks, both now seeming to be concentrating and trying to win the prize for the best poem.

An hour passed and both the girls seemed to finish their poems at the same time and put their pens down.

"Finished," they both called in agreement to their mother.

Lisa looked up from the back pages of the newspaper, as she finished scouring the NBA results from the night before and said -

"OK then girls, who wants to read their poem out first?" Both Kimmie and Sandra raised their hands at the same time, looking at each other and laughing as they tossed their hair around, eventually agreeing that Kimmie could go first - as she was the oldest - and Sandra would go second - as she was the youngest and wasn't as confident at reading out aloud as her sister was.

So, Kimmie stood up and Lisa and Sandra both sat back to listen to what she had to say.

Life on the Island
by Kimmie Matthews

We came here not so long ago,
Our Parents, my Sister and Me,
We brought our cat, he caught a rat,
And ate it by our tree.
And then I had an accident,
I fell onto the ground,
It hurt and hurt and hurt so much,

We had to leave our town.
We headed to the mainland,
Our clinic was too small,
We flew there by a helicopter,
It was big enough for all,
We had to go to hospital,
The pain it was so bad,
My mum looked after my little sister,
And I was collected by my dad.
My arm got better and less sore,
The pain it went away,
I came back to 'our' home school,
To enjoy another day.

Lisa smiled as Kimmie finished her poem and sat back down in her chair, looking very proud of herself and feeling that she had most definitely won the prize for the best poem.

"Well done Kimmie, that was an excellent account of our time here so far. So detailed, so 'poetic'." She smiled at her daughter as Sandra picked up her notebook and stood up from the table, ready to read aloud her 'piece'.

He Comes to Me at Night by Sandra Matthews

I close my eyes and grip my sheets,
He comes to me at night,
I hate the way he grinds his teeth,
He comes to me at night.
The blood stains on his overalls,
The stinky smell of breath,
He really is a scary man,
He frightens me to death,
He tells me that he loves young kids,
He comes to me at night.
His hair is very messy,
He comes to me at night.

I close my eyes so I can't see,
The man who's in my room,
If he comes to me again tonight,
I'll hit him with a broom.
Am I the only one who sees him,
I'm frightened of his bite,
Please let me sleep in another room,
He comes to me at night.

Lisa looked at Sandra, she wasn't smiling – neither of them were.

"What was that all about then?" Lisa asked, looking at her daughter, as Kimmie stared at her too, looking a little terrified at what she'd just heard come out of her sister's usually innocent mouth.

Sandra smiled a little, which was more of a grimace, as she tried to get out the words that she was trying to say.

"You asked us to write a poem about what has happened to us since we came to live here and that's the thing that makes me think of this place the most."

At that point Kimmie started to sob, not because she thought that she wasn't going to win, but because she was genuinely frightened by the poem that Sandra had written and just repeated to them out loud.

The repetition of the lines had drummed into Kimmie a sense of fear and foreboding and she wasn't looking forward to going to bed tonight now, at least her sister would be in with her though – that was something at least; but that still didn't make her feel any better.

"Where did you learn to write like that young lady, you're frightening your sister."

"The words just came to me, Emily and Hyacinth told me how to write them too" Sandra replied as she went back to her seat at the kitchen table, pulling her chair out and sitting down once more.

Lisa stared long and hard at Sandra and Kimmie, the former looking almost 'smug' and the latter, still sobbing and looking very, very worried.

"I think that's enough for todays lessons."

"But mommy, who won the poetry competition?" Piped up Sandra, believing that she must have won, due to the effect that her poem seemed to have had on everyone.

"Let's just call it a draw for now. If you kids can go to the bathroom and wash your hands, we'll start to prepare supper, your father will be home later and we need to make something really nice for him to eat."

Lisa watched as the girls got up and left the kitchen area, Sandra with a newly acquired air of superiority about her and Kimmie following in her wake, both making their way to the foot of the stairs and then up to the bathroom.

Lisa walked over to the table and picked up Sandra's poem. There was something wrong with it, it didn't even look like her handwriting – unless her written skills had improved tenfold over night. Kimmie's was the usual 'loopy' scrawl, but Sandra's appeared to be mostly written in italic, which she had never taught her or she'd never been taught in school either. The writing almost looked 'old fashioned' – like it had been written in another time, earlier than even Lisa's time at school, she would have guessed, if she hadn't seen her writing it all with her own eyes.

'And what was this with the constant references to Hyacinth and Emily? Where had they thought them up from?'

She thought to herself, as she moved back towards the kitchen sink, staring out the window and seeing a solitary magpie sitting on the windowsill.

"One for sorrow..." she said aloud, as the bird pecked at the window-pane, a fly stuck to it, no longer wriggling in a silken sticky spiders web.

Five minutes passed, then ten and then a further five and the girls had still not returned to the kitchen. Lisa looked at her watch and estimated the time that the girls should have taken to just wash their hands, one at a time and then dry them – they should've been back by now, she thought and moved to the bottom of the stairs to call them.

As she walked across the hallway heading towards the bottom of the stairs, she noticed a small puddle of water forming in the middle of the carpet and when she looked up, she noticed constant drips falling from the ceiling, beating a sodden rhythm onto the floor below.

Lisa knew that the spot on the ceiling where the water was dripping from was directly below the bathroom and so the girls must've been 'mucking about' instead of washing and drying their hands and so headed up the stairs.

Due to the possibility of water damage, Lisa took the stairs two at a time and went to open the bathroom door, which seemed to be stuck. She rattled the door handle and the door wouldn't budge, she then banged on the door and banged again.

"Girls, open the door" she shouted, almost jumping out of her skin when she heard a voice behind her say -

"We aren't in there mommy, Hyacinth and Emily are..."

Eleven

Lisa turned around to be faced with both Kimmie and Sandra, the younger daughter having already told her that they weren't in the bathroom, but their 'imaginary friends' were. The colour drained from Lisa's face as she stared at her children, who didn't even seem like her kids for a few seconds, looking more like the Grady Twins in the Stanley Kubrick filmed version of 'The Shining'. Both girls were stood staring at their mother, as she turned away from them and back to the bathroom door - which suddenly opened, without her even trying the handle again.

Lisa ran over to the sink, which was full to overflowing with water, even though the plug still appeared to be hanging on the top of the taps; something was blocking the plughole and stopping the water draining away. As she plunged her hands into the freezing cold water, she rooted around near the plug hole and pulled out a mass of hair and then some more and with one final tug, she pulled out another handful of hair and put it on the side of the sink as the water gradually began to drain away.

As the water gurgled away and the potentially ceiling ruining situation came to an end, Lisa looked at the hair and that was where the confusion began to set in. The hair was very long and dark and what made that really strange was that it was unlike the girls or anyone else's in the house. Picking up the hair, Lisa was immediately hit by the smell that came with it; the hair had a smell of burning wood about it. The odour attached smelt just like a bonfire, which made no sense as -

1) They hadn't had a fire since they'd moved in and

2) If the hair was underwater in the sink, how was it still carrying such a strong smell of burning? Shouldn't that smell have washed away under the constant flow from the taps?

Lisa turned back to the girls who were now framed in the bathroom doorway and asked –

"Where's all this strange hair come from?"

The girls looked at their mother, both stretching and twisting their fingers as they paced on the spot in the entrance to the bathroom and then both replied in unison.

"It's Hyacinth and Emily's hair, they got it burnt and were trying to wash the smell away."

Lisa looked at her daughters and started to feel like she hardly knew them. They were gradually starting to get stranger and stranger and it was beginning to unnerve her, as they both smiled back at her, as she stared at them. The water finished going down the plughole and the noise of the flow came to an end as Lisa tried to clean the sink up. She pulled more hair out of the sink and put it with the rest before dropping it into the wastebasket, to the left of the sink, between it and the toilet.

As she went back to the sink something was glinting and shining up from the plughole. The light was catching it and it seemed to look like a small shiny object, stuck too far down the drain for her to reach it, but far enough up to still catch the reflection from the lamp above. Trying to stare down the drain she got closer and it seemed to look like a piece of jewellery.

"Have you dropped one of your rings down the plughole?" she asked her daughters, both shaking their heads, again.

"Have you dropped one of my rings down there?" Again the girls shook their heads, both agreeing that they had not dropped neither theirs nor their mother's jewellery down the sink.

"Maybe it was the scary man's?" replied Sandra, looking quizzically at her mother and Kimmie nodding in total agreement.

"Stop this nonsense now. Go back downstairs and watch something on TV, I'll tidy up here and prepare supper soon."

With that, the girls marched off down the stairs and Lisa walked downstairs after them, going to the under stairs cupboard, retrieving the toolbox and making her way back up to the bathroom to investigate the lodged item on her own.

One thing that Lisa's father Bob had taught her was how to use a hammer, a screwdriver and a wrench – to the best of her abilities and it was a skill that had always stayed with her.

Going back into the bathroom, Lisa knelt down on the floor, on the rug, in front of the sink. Opening the toolbox, she pulled out the monkey wrench, which was still shining like new – it hadn't been used much at all – and started to unscrew the trap from under the sink. It was fairly tightly attached and took all of her strength to start it to unscrew, eventually it started to move and she finished the job off, loosening the nut with her hand and pulling the trap free from under the sink. As she looked into the trap, there was a further abundance of hair, but no piece of jewellery.

Going back to the toolbox, Lisa pulled out the screwdriver and crawled over to the sink on her knees, getting onto her back and going to work on dislodging whatever it was that was still stuck in the underneath of the sink. She pushed the screwdriver up into the bottom part of the drain and moved it around, more soggy hair falling out and then with a loud 'plopping' noise, the item fell out and landed on the floor next to her.

As she sat up, she picked up the shiny item that had fallen out and wiped it clean on her t-shirt. Looking at it now in the light, it was a ring, a very bright and shiny gold ring. Holding the ring up to the light, it was fairly good quality and still in a fair condition, though it looked tarnished, like it had got hot somewhere.

On further examination, Lisa could see that the top of the ring had two initials on it '**I. C.**' and on even further inspection there was an inscription written on the inside of the ring as well, in very small little letters, only just eligible to the eye. The inside of the ring said -

'Let the Little Children Come to Me and Do Not Hinder Them…'

Lisa looked at the words and knew that she had heard them somewhere before, was it a poem or something? She wasn't sure, but she popped the ring into her pocket and went back under the sink.

She reconnected the trap under the sink, tightened it up and cleaned up the puddles on the floor. Picking up the toolbox, she left the bathroom, headed back out onto the landing and made her way back downstairs. As she put the toolbox away in the under stairs cupboard, she looked over her shoulder into the lounge and could see the girls watching an episode of 'Spongebob Squarepants' – all seemed peaceful and they were both very quiet, apart from every so often when they both laughed at the cartoon.

Going back into the kitchen, Lisa retrieved her iPad from the cupboard drawer to the left of the freezer, fired it up and began to search the quote on the inside of the ring.

Within minutes she found the answer to what the quote was, it was a Bible quote from Matthew 19:14. Jesus said in the quote –

'Let the little children come to me and do not hinder them, for the Kingdom of Heaven belongs to such as these…'

'Strange quote to put in a ring' she thought to herself as she moved the ring around between her fingers, confused as to what she had found and still confused as to why it was lodged in the underside of her sink.

Looking at the clock, she realised that she had wasted longer already than she had planned and still had to make supper for them all, as Jonathan would be home shortly and at the moment they'd be eating toast if she didn't pull her finger out and make something really soon.

****

Jonathan eventually came home from work – a little late, due to having to repair several fences that had blown over in the wind. After they all ate Lisa let the girls watch some TV and then sent the girls to bed and she sat down with her husband and explained to him all about the events of the day, from the poem to the masses of hair to the ring she'd retrieved from the sink.

"Let's have a look at this ring then," Jonathan said as Lisa passed him the shiny object.

He weighed the ring up in his hand, it was of a considerable weight - for something so tiny - and appeared to be made of solid gold, not gold plated.

"Any idea on the initials or the quote?" he asked as he held the ring up to the light, making it easier to read.

"No, it's just what it is, though I did check out the quote about kids on the inside and it's from the Bible."

Jonathan clicked his lips together as he thought to himself about what it all meant and even more bizarrely, how it had ended up jammed in their sink.

"How did all the hair get in there as well?"

Lisa gave a very animated shrug of her shoulders as she bent down to put her arms around her husband and gave him a deep and very sensuous and loving hug.

Since they had moved to Martha's Vineyard they had little time for anything 'personal'. He was coming home late every day from work and she was exhausted from teaching the girls all day and then having to do all the housework as well – when she could fit it in. But this evening she was feeling lucky and as she ran her fingers through Jonathan's hair, she could see that he was getting interested as well and then, almost immediately, he jumped up, grabbed her hand and dragged her up the stairs to their bedroom, like two young kids, giddy from the chances of some time alone to themselves.

Within minutes their clothes were being rapidly discarded and strewn all over the bedroom floor and furniture. Her bra and knickers were flung off and ended up on the chair in the corner of the room, his boxers were in front of the door, next to his t-shirt and his socks finally finished up on top of the dresser next to the window. Inside five minutes they were both thrusting and moving like a well oiled machine; even though it had been a time since 'the last time', they were still a perfect fit for each other and a perfect match sexually as well as physically.

Lisa's eyes were closed as she swapped positions with Jonathan and he climbed on top, thrusting away as her eyes began to twitch and she opened them and looked at the full length mirrors on the wall to her left and that was when she saw it.

As her eyes became accustomed to the darkness she looked at the mirror and her world began to collapse.

In the mirror opposite her, she could see the reflection of her and Jonathan on the bed, but it wasn't Jonathan that was looking back. On top of her naked body was a man with unruly and greasy hair, a blue overall and badly looked after teeth and he was staring straight at her and laughing.

"Nooooooooooooooo," she screamed, making Jonathan jump up and the reflection in the mirror was him again, looking confused, very naked and erect – his erection rapidly drooping, as her scream killed the moment.

"What's the matter? What did I do wrong?"

Lisa looked at her husband and shook head, trying to shake the ghostly image out of her mind of the tramp that had been riding her like Sea Biscuit in the reflection that she'd seen.

"Nothing, I need to go to sleep," she said, as she rolled over and clenched her eyes tightly shut and within minutes she had drifted off, Jonathan at her side also snoring as he rested after a long and hard day.

Twelve

Lisa tossed and turned most of the night while her husband slept soundly. She felt bad about what had happened the night before and planned to make it up to Jonathan. As she lay there listening to the morning call of the swallows and other creatures out foraging for their breakfast, she couldn't get the vision of that horrible looking man out of her head. Did she imagine it? was she going mad?. Lisa sighed and turned to her husband. They were both still naked and Lisa wrapped her arms around his muscular body and nestled in to get some warmth. Jonathan opened his eyes to see his wife cuddling into him. He smiled and kissed her on the top of the head. Lisa looked and returned the smile,

"I love you Jonathan".

Jonathan closed his eyes and whispered "I love you" back to his wife before falling back asleep.

Kimmie and Sandra giggled as they crept into their parent's room. The sight of their parents half covered naked bodies made them laugh. Jonathan was the first to wake and realise that the children were in the room. He looked down to make sure that his modesty was covered up before acknowledging his daughters. It was far too early for his children to be thinking about that kind of stuff, but he suspected that they knew a thing or two anyways.

"Good morning kiddos",

"Good morning dad" the girls said back.

"Are you not going to work today dad?" Jonathan smiled at them and said

"No, not today girl's, I thought I would take the day off and spend it here with you lot". Jonathan had already decided the day before that he was going to stay home, after all he was his own boss, and Lisa could do with a break. Both girls cheered and scooted off back to their bedrooms to get dressed.

Jonathan had woken Lisa up by running his fingers down the curves of her body, he was aware that he was unable to follow through with his teasing because of the girls, but it didn't stop him. Lisa gasped a gentle sigh as she felt her husband's fingers gently stroke the soft mound of hair that was just below her stomach. Lisa opened her eyes and stretched. Jonathan leaned forward and kissed her on the lips.

"Morning beautiful" he said with a mischievous smile. Lisa wrapped her arms around him and returned the compliment.

"The kids are already awake," Jonathan, said, "After all it is almost seven thirty".

Lisa jumped up out of the bed, "

Jonathan, you're late for work".

"Relax, I am staying home today". Lisa grinned, and although she wasn't religious, she was thankful that she was blessed with such a loving, caring husband.

After a few minutes, Kimmie came in all dressed, she had her white dress with the magnolias on that she had gotten for her birthday, and was sporting a white glittery pair of tights and white and red sandals.

"Wow, don't you look pretty" Lisa said.

"Go on give us a twirl," Jonathan said with an air of fun in his voice. Kimmie smiled and twirled her dress around as if she was in a fashion show. Lisa looked as her daughter waved her dress in the air, and then she noticed something odd, out of place on her daughters dress.

"Kimmie, come here my darling I want to see you."

Lisa wrapped a blanket around herself to hide her protruding breasts before asking her youngest daughter to turn around. All the blood seemed to drain from Lisa's face. It quickly went from rosy red cheeks to a grey sickly gaunt looking old woman. Lisa was horrified. On the back of Kimmie's dress, down by her buttocks, Lisa could see four black oily fingerprints smeared across the back as if someone or something had grabbed her from behind.

Lisa said to Kimmie in her stern voice,

"Go and change that dress please Kimmie",

"But..." before Kimmie even had the chance to finish asking her question, Lisa had already snapped at her. Kimmie turned and walked away back into her bedroom.

Jonathan sat up in the bed, he had a concerned look upon his face and he had started biting his bottom lip, a long since forgotten habit that had not shown its head in years.

"Lisa, what the hell was that all about?"

Lisa put her head in her hands and felt ashamed for snapping at her daughter the way she did. Jonathan knew then that the pressure of the move and the home schooling was starting to take its toll on his wife, or so he thought. Lisa looked at her husband with sorrow in her eyes. Sandra walked into the bedroom and handed Lisa Kimmie's dress.

"Here you go mom, but we don't know how the black stain got there?"

Lisa took the dress off her daughter and examined the black oily smear that was on the back of it. They certainly resembled fingerprints but she was unsure as to how it got there. Jonathan took the dress and looked at it closely.

"You know what darling, it may have been me the other night when I went in to kiss them goodnight, my hands still had oil on them from the generator."

Lisa stared at the stains and said

"Ok. I will wash it again today."

With that Jonathan had somehow managed to get his pants on without his daughters copping an eyeful and jumped out of bed.

"Who's for breakfast?" both Lisa and Sandra smiled and both in unison said,

"Me, me, me".

It was a fine day and once Jonathan had finished making a hearty breakfast of pancakes and toast, he said to Lisa and the girls to get their coats on as they were going out for a family walk. That was the beauty of living in such beautiful surroundings. Sandra and Kimmie were excited, although they like doing school work with their mother, they would much prefer to be out adventuring in the woods with their father. Lisa packed a rucksack with some sandwiches and a drink for everyone and the four of them left for their walk.

Sandra loved the outdoors, especially being in the woods. She always thought it mysterious and magical. There was an abundance of wildlife to discover and both girls were trying to name as many animals as possible. Lisa held on to Jonathan's hand and took in a deep lungful of fresh woodland air. She was in no doubt now that they had made the right decision to move out here. It was breath taking. Both girls were happy foraging in the bushes and among the trees for whatever creatures they could find. As they continued on deeper into the woods, the narrow dirt track came to a crossroads. To the right was a track that would lead them to the outer perimeter of the woods and to the left brought them further into the middle of the dense woodland. Sandra had already made her mind up which way they were going to go, and skipped away happily to the left with her sister following not far behind her.

"Not too far in front girls, stay where we can see you", came their mother's voice.

"Ok mom" said Sandra as she waded into the undergrowth.

Kimmie was busy collecting various flowers and had been busy pulling at some wild primrose to give to Lisa. Jonathan and Lisa walked over to where she was. Kimmie handed Lisa a ragged bunch of yellow and deep purple primrose.

"Here you go mom, they are for you" both Lisa and Jonathan smiled at each other and almost subconsciously knew that they were good parents.

The scream echoed and bounced off the trees. Both Jonathan and Lisa screamed

"Sandra" at the same time and immediately turned to see where she was.

She was stood about ten feet into the far side of the track and was frozen stiff and shaking. Jonathan ran across to her fearing that she had been bitten by a snake or a spider.

"Sandra, what's the matter darling, what's wrong?"

Jonathan knelt down beside her and grabbed her by the shoulders,

"What's wrong Sandra."

She turned to look at her father and then looked forward again pointing to something that was strewn in the bushes. Jonathan looked over to see a dirty faded blue pair of overalls, with rips down the sides as if somebody or something had mauled at it with ferocious force. Dry bloodstains smeared the rotting garment.

"Oh kiddo, it's just an old pair of discarded overalls, there's nothing to be scared of".

Sandra looked at her father and shook her head,

"No dad, it's not the pants, look there," she said pointing to something else further back.

Jonathan looked again. Shivers raced down his spine as his heart beat like a train gathering speed. Under a large clump of fern, a human skull protruded from beneath the soil.

Thirteen

Lisa held Sandra and Kimmie's hands as they made their way back to the house. Nobody was really talking and there was a sense of urgency in their step. Once they had reached the house, Jonathan instructed the girls to go wash up and change their clothes. Without hesitation they both made their way up the stairs.

"That's given me the creeps" Lisa said, "What are we going to do about it?"

Jonathan looked at his wife, his expression was blank and he was looking tired.

"I'll phone the sheriff and let him know what we have found; he more than likely will want me to show him exactly where it is."

Lisa hated the idea of a dead man at the back of her house.

"I wouldn't read too much into it Lisa, there are hundreds of ancient burials scattered around these parts".

Somehow deep inside Lisa didn't share her husband's optimism.

Jonathan poured himself a fresh glass of orange juice and sat at the kitchen table with the phone in his hand.

"I'll just go check on the kids," said Lisa.

Jonathan nodded to her as he Googled the number for the sheriff's office. After a couple of rings, an officer Martinez answered the phone.

"Woods Hole Police department, how may I help you?"

Her voice sounded well rehearsed, as no doubt she has said that line hundreds of times before.

"Hello, my name is Jonathan Matthews, I am the forest manager for the Eden group, and I want to report the discovery of a human skull not far from Eden lodge".

"Ok sir can you please tell me whereabouts you have seen this skull?"

Jonathan paused for a moment while officer Martinez continued to input the data on her system.

"It's about a twenty five minute hike from our lodge, my daughter stumbled across it while we were out walking earlier today".

Officer Martinez stopped typing and went silent for a moment.

"Ok Mr. Matthews we will have somebody come out to you today and we will take it from there".

"Thank you" Jonathan said before ending the call.

Rex the cat had wandered into the kitchen just as Jonathan was finishing the last of his orange juice. His gentle purrs and erected tail wafted gently in the afternoon's air.

Lisa had come down the stairs to make the girls a drink, and walked into the kitchen. Suddenly and without warning, Rex arched his back and hissed, his claws like daggers gripping onto the rug and staring like a rattlesnake ready to strike at Lisa.

Lisa stopped dead in her tracks to study the cat.

Rex let out a deep throaty gurgling sound and pounced. Lisa didn't have time to react before Rex's claws slashed at her face.

Jonathan jumped up from the table and dived at the cat grabbing it by its tail. Rex turned his head and sank his teeth deep into Jonathan's right hand. It hurt like a sonofabitch and Jonathan yelped in agony. Rex landed beside the sink and hissed again, this time he was concentrating on the far corner by the food cupboard. Something had spooked the cat into attack mode. Rex turned and leapt onto the sink and scuttled out the opened kitchen window.

By now Sandra and Kimmie had come down the stairs to see what all the commotion was about. Seeing their parents covered in blood scared them into tears. Lisa was sat at the table with a cloth on her cheek trying to stem the flow of blood that was oozing from the four scratches on her face. Jonathan was by the sink running his hand under the cold tap. Sweat bubbled down his forehead and he looked flushed in the face.

"Mom, Dad, what's happened?" Kimmie said in her innocent terrified voice.

Both Lisa and Jonathan looked at each other before Jonathan said that everything was ok, they just had an accident. The air inside the lodge seemed to have changed. No longer did it feel bright and airy but more heavy and muggy. It felt like a huge depression had somehow materialised without them realising it. Sandra looked at her mother and went over and hugged her.

"It's ok Mommy, Emily and Hyacinth are beside you."

Lisa turned to look at her daughter, she was smiling but her eyes were a saddened shade of blue. The coldness crept up on her. Although it must have been at least forty degrees in the kitchen Lisa was shivering. She felt an icy breath on the back of her hair and jumped when an unknown voice whispered into her ear.

"Isaiah Clevedon…"

Jonathan asked her was she ok as Lisa's face turned a deathly hew of grey. She looked at her husband and blurted out the two words that were whispered to her,

"Isaiah Clevedon."

The two girls went back upstairs to play in their bedroom, while Lisa and Jonathan finished cleaning themselves up. Not long after the cat incident, a police car pulled up and parked on the little bit of grass in the yard. Two police officers stepped out of the car and made their way to the front door. Jonathan went out to meet them.

"Mr Matthews",

"Yes sir," Jonathan said and extended his injured hand, which now sported a nice pink and blue bandage.

"I'm Sherriff Dawson, and this is officer Martinez."

Jonathan wondered if it was the same officer Martinez who he spoke with on the phone earlier.

"I believe you have stumbled across a human skull".

"Yes sir in the woods, I'll just grab my boots and I will take you to it". Jonathan kissed Lisa on the cheek and left for the woods again with the Sheriff and the officer.

It wasn't long before the three of them made their way to where the skull was. Jonathan pointed the Sheriff to the clump of ferns and said

"It's under there."

Martinez remained quiet and panned the area for other potential bones before noticing the faded blue blood stained overalls in the bush. She bent down and picked them up and studied what was left of them. It was obvious they had been there quite a while due to the condition they were in, but she examined them nonetheless. Sheriff Dawson pulled back the ferns and sure enough, there it was. The skull was half covered in mud, its eye sockets protruding out of the ground and staring into their very souls.

Martinez ran her fingers over the manky overalls and gasped. This not only alerted Jonathan but the Sherriff too. Jonathan looked at her quizzically as she held the overalls in her hand. Sheriff Dawson walked over and both of them examined the overalls.

Jonathan looked on at Dawson and Martinez and wondered what they were looking at. As he glanced down at the garment Jonathan could see the remnants of embroidery, he could just barely see the initials, I.C sewn into the top pocket.

Dawson instructed Martinez to bag the overalls up before talking to Jonathan.

"There's nothing to worry about Mr Matthews, this particular skull is that of a native Indian, and is clearly a couple of hundred years old at least."

Jonathan was no archaeologist and took the Sheriff's word for it. "The best thing to do is to leave it in place and not to disturb it, it is part of a sacred Indian burial, and there are hundreds around these parts".

But little did Jonathan know. The sheriff and officer Martinez were clearly spooked by something.

"From this grave I shall return, in the dead of night to make them burn".

Fourteen

Back at the lodge, Lisa was sat at the dining room table, the four scratches across her cheek had stopped bleeding already, but they were still painful; the stinging wasn't as bad as the feeling of foreboding that she was sensing in their right home now.

"Who the hell was it that spoke to me earlier and who on earth is Isaiah Clevedon?" She thought to herself as she dabbed at the wound, the blood was dry and the weeping had almost stopped now as well.

And then it all clicked in.

Lisa put her hand into her jeans pocket and pulled out the ring that she'd retrieved and held it up on her outstretched palm.

The initials on the top of the ring were 'I.C'; was it too much of a coincidence that the words whispered into her ear were 'Isaiah Clevedon?' It seemed to be much too much of a chance occurrence and as the front door clicked behind her, she turned around to see Jonathan coming back in and closely followed by the two members of the local police force.

Officer Martinez and Sherriff Dawson came in with her husband and stood to the left of the doorway as Jonathan shut the door behind them and went on to explain to Lisa what they had actually found.

"Well I've shown the Sherriff and Officer Martinez, where we found the skull and they've kindly explained to me what it probably is." He began, trying to be a little relaxed as he told Lisa what he'd been informed.

"There are hundreds of Indian burial grounds around here and the skull that we found, on our walk, is probably over a couple hundred years old, so there's nothing for us to really worry about."

Lisa looked at Jonathan as he tried to not connect with her stare, as he looked around the room, his eyes eventually landing back on the police by the doorway.

"That was right wasn't it?"

"Yes, Mr Matthews," replied Sherriff Dawson, "There's nothing at all to worry about and we'll leave the skull where you found it, best not to cause any '*dark elements*' or '*mumbo-jumbo*' from ancient history to be dragged up. The overalls we'll burn though; they're probably from the people who were working here a few years ago laying the pipeline to your home - for the sewage system - they left such a mess on the island."

Still staring at her husband, Lisa could see that he didn't exactly believe all of this explanation and he was tugging at his ear, which he always did when he was confused or stressed or sometimes both.

"If the company had staff making such a mess here and aiding to the destruction of the local environment, can't we go back to them? We do know the initials of the employee at least, which should help."

"What were the initials?" asked Lisa, as she rubbed the ring in her pocket, waiting for the inevitable.

"I.C" replied Jonathan.

As Lisa turned to the Sherriff and his colleague, she noticed that they both appeared to be looking very uncomfortable with how this investigation was going. What had started, as a 'usual' call out, was turning into something much more and Sherriff Dawson, began to wheeze and cough, his asthma starting to kick in.

"Are you ok," Lisa asked as she pulled the ring out of her pocket and held it up.

The Sherriff stopped panting and glared at Martinez, both sweating and looking worried. The look on his face said *'let's leave'* but his feet seemed to be ignoring his brains order, as if they were willing to stay and sort out this case, even if his body wasn't.

"I.C. are the initials on this ring," Lisa said as she walked over to them, holding her hand aloft.

"Perhaps it's just a coincidence? Lots of people have the same initials as that." Said Martinez, as her partner stared at Lisa, his eyes transfixed on the ring in her hand, almost rendering him speechless.

The light shone on the ring and it almost seemed to light up the room, but not with a bright and summery light, but with a dark light – if such a thing was possible.

Martinez was the least confused of the two and asked the question that was on both of their lips –

"Where did you find the ring? Was that in the woods as well?"

Lisa stopped in front of the two members of her local law enforcement team and held the ring between her fingers, rolling it around as it caught the light shining in the window. The ring kept the gaze of both of them, like it was hypnotising the only two people in the room who may have known more than they appeared to be willing to spill.

"I found the ring jammed tight in the plughole of our bathroom, that and an abundance of dark hair. Whoever lived here before didn't believe in leaving the place tidy before they went and…"

"Well they didn't have a chance did they…" interrupted Martinez, for which she got a swift elbow in the ribs from the Sherriff, as he frowned at her, as if to say *'shut the fuck up now, before we tell them too much.'*

"Ok, we need to move on now. We will keep you updated on anything regarding your find" said Sherriff Dawson and with that the two turned on their heel, left via the front door, climbed into their patrol car and drove off as fast as if they were heading to the nearest doughnut store, five minutes before closing time.

"I think tomorrow we'll do some investigating of our own" said Lisa as she stood in the lounge, popping the ring back in her pocket for safe-keeping.

Jonathan just stood and stared at her and their kids carried on colouring in their drawings at the kitchen table, oblivious to anything that had just taken place.

Fifteen

Getting up at 7am, Lisa slipped out of the bed and walked naked towards their en-suite bathroom.

The house was incredibly, quiet for that time of the morning. Jonathan was still snoring, deep in sleep and no sounds at all were coming from the girl's room. The only noise was the gentle slapping of Lisa's bare feet as she walked across the polished wooden floorboards of the bedroom and onto the tiled floor of the bathroom, where the tone of her footsteps changed and she shuddered slightly as the tiles were so cold.

Lisa went to the toilet and spent five minutes on her own, sitting down and contemplating, thinking about what she would be spending her day doing. She already had a plan and discussed it with Jonathan the night before. It had been decided – between them – that she would go into town and visit the local newspaper, to ask a few questions, in hope of gaining some answers and being able to move forward with their lives. Jonathan would stay at home and look after the girl's and she would try to get some closure on the strange events that hard started happening since they had moved into their house.

As she pulled the flush, she stood up and walked over to the white enamel sink unit. She looked at her reflection in the mirror; she was looking old. The last few nights she hadn't slept well and the voices, the images, the skull – had all started to take their toll on her and the lack of sleep was making her look older, even after such a short period of time.

Then she thought she saw something pass behind her, reflected in the mirror. She turned around and their was nothing there, but it was definitely one of those moments, when you think that you catch something out of the corner of your eye and then it's gone.

Lisa turned her head back to the mirror and rubbed her eyes with the heels of hands, trying to remove any nonsense from her head.

'I'm going slightly mad...' she thought to herself, recalling the song by Queen and the video where Freddie Mercury – their lead singer - had started to look ill, from his battle with HIV; she wasn't that haggered yet, but she felt exhausted and it would be a shower that would drag her into the new day and hopefully invigorate her aching and tired limbs.

Leaning into the bath – behind the shower curtain – she turned on the taps and flipped the indicator from bath to shower and a steady stream of water began to flow downstairs, gravity dragging it all eventually towards the plughole.

As she watched the water cascading down, she noticed that it wasn't emptying and it was gradually beginning to fill up and not drain away. Lisa bent down to the plughole – which was now submerged under a few inches of warm water – and routed around with her hand, pulling at what was stuck there, her hand coming out of the water with a mass of long black hair, just like she had found blocking the sink in the family bathroom.

"Yuck!" she squealed, throwing the clump of hair into the wastebasket to the left of the toilet.

"This is just ridiculous," she said out loud as she watched the water eventually beginning to disappear in the bath. Within a few seconds the final puddles of water in the bath were gurgling down the drain, as they were replaced by more water surging down from the showerhead above.

Pulling back the curtain and climbing in, Lisa allowed the warm liquid to waterfall over her shoulders as she rubbed shower gel into her body, lathering up her breasts and torso, as she closed her eyes and made the most of her five minutes of relaxing piece.

A hand then began to caress the back of her neck, as she stood there, with her back to the shower curtain.

'I must have woken Jonathan up' she thought to herself as the hand continued to stroke and smooth around the base of her neck, a second

hand then starting to rub her right shoulder in a very comforting circular motion, her eyes shut in relaxation.

Then the movement changed…

Before she could do anything, the soft and gentle hands became strong and leathery talons as they both slipped up and onto her neck, putting pressure on her larynx as they began to strangle her.

With each movement, the grip increased and the compression intensified, as she started to feel herself gasping for air, her mouth filling with water, as her head was tilted backwards, under the spray from above.

Coughing and spitting she tried to push Jonathan out of the way, opening her eyes and turning around she was met by the man that she had seen before in the bedroom mirror – the man who had unkempt hair, bad teeth and a blue overall - as she stared she noticed the 'initials' embroidered on them – I.C.

As he leant forward he whispered in her ear – barely audible over the sound of rushing water –

"Isaiah loves a moist bit of you, but he loves your little girls, so much, much more…"

With that, the grip on her neck was released and she slid down the shower to lay in the bath, the water still pouring down on her head – her hair hanging damp in her eyes. As she looked up, there was once more no one there and she was alone in her en-suite – she could even still hear Jonathan snoring from the bedroom and deathly silence from the girl's room.

"Oh my god, the girls," she screamed as clambered out of the bath and ran into their room to make sure the man hadn't gone in there, her feet slipping and sliding on the polished floorboards as she made her way along the hallway to the girls bedroom.

"Mommie your naked," laughed Kimmie as she pointed at her mother, who was standing in the door to their room with no clothes on.

"Oh my," exclaimed Sandra as she began laughing and giggling and pointing at her, from her bed.

"Did anyone come in here girls? In the last couple minutes?"

Kimmie and Sandra looked at each other and both said together –

"Only Hyacinth and Emily."

In total exasperation, Lisa blurted out the first things on her mind and shouted - “Not your stupid make believe friends, but a man in overalls, that we don’t know.”

“But they aren’t ‘make believe friends. Only because they don’t talk to you or dad, doesn’t make them not real,” replied Sandra, staring at her mother’s naked form for long enough to make her mom feel embarrassed and head back to the bathroom for her towel.

Seconds later, Lisa was back in the girls bedroom and berating them for talking such nonsense, whilst all the time she was thinking to herself about what had happened to her in the en-suite and the voice that she’d heard; there was certainly something not quite right about this house.

****

Half an hour passed and Lisa had already left the girls room, gone back to hers and got dressed. She went back into the girl’s room and neither of them were there, the beds were a mess and toys were strewn all over the floor and it was then – as she picked up some of the toys to put away - that she heard their voices talking and giggling from the kitchen downstairs.

Walking downstairs, the girls carried on chatting to each other in the kitchen and when she actually entered the room, they were both sat at the table, eating cereal, drawing and colouring; some of the loose sheets of paper spread across the kitchen table already damp from the spilt puddles of milk.

“Is everything ok girls?” she cautiously asked as she picked up a cloth and wiped up the milk and threw the soggy bits of paper in the kitchen bin.

“All good Mommie” they both said in near stereo and went back to their drawings.

BANG, BANG, BANG, BANG…

Lisa spun around to the knock on their front door, making her jump, her nerves already on edge.

Walking to the door, she looked back at the girls who appeared to be unaware of anything strange in the house.

As she opened the door wide, she was greeted by the sight of Officer Martinez, this time in her 'civvies' – a figure hugging t-shirt, faded blue and a pair of scuffed sneakers; she looked every part the casual member of the community, on a day off work.

"Hi, can I come in, I have something to tell you."

Lisa moved out of the way ushering her visitor in.

"Can I get you a drink? Or a bite to eat Officer Martinez?"

Martinez shook her head and replied. "No, I'm fine and you can call me Brandi – I'm not on duty at the moment." With that she walked past Lisa and into the lounge, pacing slowly up and down in front of the sofa.

"I need to tell you a little bit about your home," she began, trying to break into a smile, but struggling to get the corners of her mouth to turn up, as if they were in a facial protest at what she was about to divulge.

"Strange things have occurred hear over the years and the people who have lived at the property have not stayed here very long, in fact the person who lived here last has never been the same again."

Lisa sat down on the sofa, as Brandi continued her constant movement 'to and fro' across the length of the room.

"Only a year ago, Jeffrey Walsh moved in here, to do the same job that your husband has now," she started, clenching and unclenching her hands as she spoke. "But he didn't last very long."

Watching Brandi Martinez speak about what had happened to the previous occupant of their home was difficult, as she seemed to be struggling to put the story into words. Her face contorted several times as she carried on with a brief history of events, trying to get Lisa 'up to speed'.

"We had several calls from Mr Walsh about intruders on his property, over the course of 6 months – up to when he had to leave," she started, her nerves still evident.

"He claimed that two children kept breaking into the house and running around in here at night, which was keeping him awake. He called us numerous times over the last few days before he was taken away."

"Taken away?"

"Yes, he was found wandering around outside the house with a rifle, randomly shooting into the woods around the perimeter, crying and sobbing, like I've never seen a man act before. He was struggling to make any sense when the ambulance arrived and they took him to the care home in town, where he's been ever since."

"What did he tell you about the children?" asked Lisa.

Brandi looked Lisa straight in the eyes and said "he said that the children had spoken to him in the night and that they had come to warn him about Isaiah..."

Sixteen

After Brandi had finished relaying the particulars of past events at their home and had subsequently left, Lisa sat down at the table. She was quiet and deep in thought. Kimmie and Sandra were still in their pyjamas and were finishing up with their colouring.

"What do you think of our pictures mommy?" Kimmie said handing her the sheet of coloured in A4 paper.

Lisa rubbed at her temple with her forefinger and took the sheet from her daughter. Both girls had drawn the same picture. Lisa looked at the pictures and immediately she had a sick feeling in the pit of her stomach. There were three adults and four children, yet one of the adults was coloured in complete black, almost shadow-like. Underneath each figure were their names, Mommy, Daddy, Kimmie, Sandra, Hyacinth, Emily and the last one which stunned Lisa into a state of shock, the bad man. Lisa looked at her girls, the two of them, in their innocence, were oblivious to what they had just shown her.

"Girls, listen to me now," Lisa said in a calm but stern voice, "who is this bad man in the pictures?" Both girls looked at each other and said in unison,

"The bad man mommy. We have not seen him, Emily and Hyacinth have told us about him, and what he looks like, he is not a very nice man at all."

By now, Lisa was certain that there was more to her daughter's imaginary friends.

"Ok" Lisa said, "And what does this bad man do to make him bad?"

For a moment, Lisa felt like the worst mother in the world for subjecting her daughters to such vulgarities. Kimmie looked at her mother and said in her innocent child-like voice,

" He hurts kids."

Lisa was stunned in shock. A sudden wave of dread filled her from her feet to the top of her head. She needed to find out everything she could about this house and their other occupants, and quickly, she thought to herself.

"Right girls go and get dressed".

Both girls jumped down from the table and happily made their way upstairs to their bedrooms to get dressed. Lisa could hear Sandra humming a tune she had heard somewhere, as she climbed the stairs.

By now, Jonathan was awake and was already showered and dressed. He kissed both girls on their heads and headed down the stairs to the kitchen. Lisa was sat at the table staring at the pictures with a worried look on her face.

"What's the matter, Lisa, you look like you've seen a ghost," Jonathan said.

Lisa drew her eyes up from the pictures and handed them to her husband,

"I think you may be right Jonathan," she said. Jonathan took the pictures and looked at them.

After reading the names underneath the characters, he placed them on the counter and made himself a coffee.

"Well!" Lisa said in a slightly raised voice. Jonathan sat down at the table with his coffee.

"Well what" he said, as he began sipping from the cup.

"Oh come on, do you not find this too much of a coincidence, first the ring, then the overalls, and now our daughters drawing ghosts in their pictures, and how do you explain what happened to Mr. Walsh?"

"Listen, darling; I am sure there is a perfectly reasonable explanation for all of this and that you are getting yourself worked up into a state for n reason."

Jonathan was a non-believer in ghosts and ghouls and all that goes bump in the night and always tried to rationalise things.

The air within the house had slowly become heavier, more oppressive and Lisa suspected that it was taking a toll on her husband, but he was too stubborn to admit it. Jonathan was a good man, and she loved him with all her heart, but his stubbornness sometimes formed a rift between them.

Lisa sat back in the chair and shook her head. She was not happy, and Jonathan knew this. Lisa knew it was pointless arguing the toss with her husband and asked if he would look after the children while she popped into town. She knew he was taking another day off work and had planned to make the most of it. Jonathan smiled and said,

"I love you, of course I will".

Lisa forced herself to smile back and repeated back the three words she had just heard. She was about to tell him what had happened to her in the shower earlier that morning, but for some reason decided not to, she needed evidence, written proof that something was happening with this house.

Lisa kissed her husband goodbye and waved to the children who were watching her from the bedroom window. She started the station wagon and headed down the dirt track that led to the road into town. As she was nearing the bend, she glanced in the mirror to look back at the house. Just for a second, she thought she could see an image of a young girl dressed in old-time clothes waving back at her from the front of the house, but when she blinked it was gone.

The weather was overcast but remained very warm, and Lisa had the window down to let some fresh air into the old car. The journey into town would only take about twenty minutes or so, and she was looking forward to it. Her first stop was the grocery store; she needed to get all of the household stuff done first before she began any research into the lodge and this so-called Isaiah Clevedon.

After parking up outside the store, Lisa made her way inside the shop. It wasn't a very big store, but it was sufficient for the size of the town. She grabbed a trolley and made her way slowly down the narrow aisles, browsing at the selection of food it had on offer. Lisa stopped at the bakery section and was debating whether or not to get three loaves of bread or two when she heard whispering coming from behind the stacked shelves in front of her. She glanced up and peered in between the gaps of the shelves.

Two women around the late fiftyish mark, one with long hair in a ponytail and the other with a headscarf on, who clearly was recovering from chemotherapy as her cheeks were sunken, and her eyes were brow less, already she looked like a walking corpse, a telltale sign of the treatment for cancer, were speaking in hushed voices.

Lisa could hear their conversation quite clearly as they were talking about their children. Lisa thought to herself their kids must be grown up by now, but by the way they were talking it sounded as if they were quite young. The woman with the long hair had a tone of anger to her voice as she talked highly about how old her daughter would have been today. Lisa realised that her daughter must have died, and today was her birthday.

It was a sad thing to hear, and a lump formed in her throat which she had to swallow, she thought about her own children, and if anything ever happened to them she doubted she would have the strength to carry on. Then the conversation took a darker more sinister course.

The woman with the long hair almost growled as she spat out the words,

"If it wasn't for that sick Bastard, she would still be alive today, he took my beautiful sweet Mary away from me."

The cancer woman hugged her and said in an almost apologetic tone,

"It wasn't just your daughter, we all felt the wrath of that monster."

But before Lisa had time to fully process what she was hearing, came the kicker, the salt to the wound. The woman with the ponytail clenched her fist angrily and growled the words,

"Damn you to hell Isaiah Clevedon".

Lisa's heart skipped a beat, realising that her daughter was murdered was hard enough, but from what Lisa could gather, Isaiah Clevedon was a bitter pill to swallow.

"Oh my God."

The words seemed to stab Lisa right through the heart, it made her feel weak, and she thought she was going to collapse there and then in the middle of the aisle. Lisa quickly composed herself and hurried around to where the two women were.

"Excuse me, ladies, I am sorry for my intrusion, my name is Lisa Matthews, I live out at Eden lodge with my husband and two children, I couldn't help but overhear your conversation, and my apologies for eavesdropping, but you have mentioned a name, Isaiah Clevedon".

Both women looked at each other in shock at what Lisa was asking them.

"Can you tell me more about him please?"

The healthier of the two women shook her head and turned away, but not before telling Lisa to '*back the fuck off and leave things be*'. She grabbed her friend's arm, and the two women hurried out of the store. Lisa felt numb. Now she was convinced something sinister was going on and this Isaiah Clevedon was smack bang in the middle. Lisa was determined to get to the bottom of it.

Seventeen

Lisa grabbed what shopping she thought they needed and quickly threw the groceries into the trolley. She wanted to get out of the store as quickly as possible so hurried along to the cashier. After paying with her credit card she left the store and loaded up the car. Lisa needed a moment or two to process what was happening so decided to sit in the front seat to gather her thoughts.

She needed a plan of action; she needed to find out as much as possible about this so-called Isaiah Clevedon and what his connection to her home was.

After a few minutes passed, Lisa got out of the station wagon and slammed the door shut behind her. Her first port of call was the local newspaper if anybody was going to have information about this Isaiah character it was going to be the local rag. Lisa headed off in the direction of the town centre to find the main office for the Haven Herald newspaper.

It wasn't long before she saw the sign for the newspaper. It's huge lettering in black and red, was written in a gothic style, giving it an old authentic look. Lisa headed towards the building and didn't hesitate before going in.

The main reception to the offices was draped in a bold cream and black decor. Various awards hung on the walls surrounding the reception desk; no doubt they were internal awards as the town itself, was far too small to have won any major awards.

A small aquarium with various fish, stood in the centre by the far wall, with a picture of what Lisa could only think was one of the founding members hanging with pride above the glass tank.

Lisa walked over to the reception desk and stood in line behind a small man with greying hair and neatly ironed grey slacks, who was chatting with the receptionist about placing an advert for his local computer business.

After a couple of minutes, the man, who Lisa couldn't help but hear, was A.J. Carson, of 'Carson Computers', turned and smiled at her. He was a pleasant-looking kind of guy, with a small-reddened birthmark on the left-hand side of his head, and thick round-rimmed glasses that hung down on the tip of his nose. He could have easily passed as a teacher or a Lawyer. He bid farewell to the receptionist and said good day to Lisa as he passed by. Lisa smiled and acknowledged him with a nod of her head.

Lisa said, good morning to the receptionist and introduced herself. The receptionist aptly named Ronnie Rydall, smiled back at Lisa and returned the gratuity,

"How may I help you, Mrs. Matthews?"

Ronnie was a fine looking woman in her late twenties, and Lisa couldn't help but notice her voluptuous breasts, the white short-sleeved blouse stretched over her mounds causing the seams to gape open at the side. Lisa found it very off-putting and tried her best not to stare.

"Hi I am wondering if you may be able to help me? I live up at Eden Lodge, and I am just doing a little research into the history of the place, I am hoping that you may be able to point me in the right direction."

Ronnie smiled back at Lisa to reveal a perfect set of pearly white teeth, smeared with a hint of her dark red lipstick that she was wearing.

'Well' said Ronnie, I can certainly search on the paper's database for you to see if it has been mentioned at all?"

"Oh that would be fantastic thank you so much" Lisa said.

Again Ronnie smiled and began typing into the computer database for Eden Lodge.

The two women didn't speak while the computer finished generating the results of the search. Ronnie scrolled down through the page and stopped at an article, which read, 'Flood at Eden Lodge'; she shook her head and carried on down the screen. Eventually, she stopped at an early article dating back to the 1800s.

"Oh here is one that may be of interest," she said.

She clicked on the article and immediately in big black letters across the screen was "Death at the Lodge".

"Would you like me to read it out to you, or if you prefer I can print a copy off for you".

Curiosity had gotten the better of Lisa at that point and kindly asked the receptionist to do both. Ronnie began reading the article that bore the date September 26, 1863.

Fire Destroys Lodge,

'The tragedy occurred yesterday at Eden Lodge, when fire broke out in the early hours of Saturday morning, killing all four members of the Jones Family. The occupants, Henry and Georgette Jones, and their two children Emily and Hyacinth had all succumbed to the inferno.'

Lisa's mouth gaped open and a sudden wave of ice-cold chills coursed up and down her body.

"The girls" she said in a fractured voice to the receptionist, who by now was aware that Lisa was in some distress.

"I know" Ronnie said, "but you have to realise this happened well over a century ago."

The sound of the printer whirring into life revived Lisa back to some form of normality. She now knew whom her girls were speaking to back at their home. Ronnie handed Lisa the sheet of paper with the article on it, once again Lisa stared at the print.

"Shall I continue Mrs. Matthews?"

Lisa looked up from the paper and said,

"Please do."

Ronnie carried on scrolling down through the rest of the search results and stopped at anything she felt might be relevant to Lisa's enquiry. After a couple of minutes of clicking different articles, Ronnie stopped once again on an article, which read.

'Mystery Intruders at Eden Lodge'.

The article itself was only dated last year, and it cemented the information that Brandi Martinez said about the former occupant of Eden Lodge, Jeffrey Walsh. Lisa asked Ronnie to print the article out once again. No other search results jumped out from the screen or had any historical relevance. Lisa thanked Ronnie for all her help and turned to leave the office.

Then Lisa thought, in her haste, she had forgotten all about Isaiah Clevedon.

"Oh one last thing please Ronnie." Both women had established a first name basis earlier on in their first conversation,

"Can you do one last search for me, can you search the name Isaiah Clevedon for me please?"

Ronnie's eyes widened upon hearing that name. She started to shift awkwardly in her chair, and her whole demeanor had changed drastically.

Ronnie now had a scared look upon her face, giving her a child-like visage; Lisa became aware she was uncomfortable. Ronnie gave a forced grin and typed the name Isaiah Clevedon into her computer. Ronnie already knew what the search results would hold on him.

Little did Lisa know Ronnie herself was a victim of the monster that was Isaiah Clevedon.

Like a true professional, Ronnie composed herself and printed off at least half a dozen articles all relating to Isaiah Clevedon. She did not attempt to read any of the articles out to Lisa, and Lisa, feeling the shift in friendliness didn't ask her to.

Ronnie handed Lisa, the pile of articles with a shaky hand. Once again Lisa thanked her for all her help and that she hoped to meet her again one day, in a less formal environment. Ronnie smiled again, flashing her perfect teeth and said 'likewise'.

Lisa glanced down at her watch, it was almost 4 pm and it was starting to get dark outside. She hurried along back to where she had parked the car and sat in silence for a few moments. Her emotions were numb from what she had just found out about the Jones family, but more to the point she had some evidence now to show her husband, once she got back home.

Eighteen

The sun was slowly setting over Eden Lodge and Jonathan was outside raking up the leaves that appeared to be dropping in their hundreds in the last few days as Autumn changed to Winter and the evenings began to draw in. The temperature had also dropped in the last few days and Halloween was just on the horizon, dragging its spooky daylong carcass into view, coming to scare the children and cost the adults of Martha's Vineyard in new costumes and candy.

The girls were once again sitting in the kitchen - at the table – drawing and colouring pictures together, peaceful and content in each other's company.

As the leaves were piled up into manageable 'clumps', more leaves fell and Jonathan had to start to scrape them up into piles as well.

And then the wind suddenly picked up.

With an unexpected gust, all the leaves in the backyard and front-yard of the property were blown into the air, as a mini tornado swept around the property and messed up all of Jonathan's handy-work.

"Fuck, fuck, fuckity, FUCK!" cursed Jonathan as the property looked in a worse state than it had before he'd started, just over an hour ago.

As he looked around the front of the lodge, he saw the girls waving and laughing at the kitchen window – they'd seen the leaves blowing around and they both seemed to find it hilarious.

Looking at the girls as they giggled, Jonathan couldn't help but laugh himself; they certainly made life worth living and their chuckling really was quite addictive and always made him and Lisa crack up, with them both ending up laughing too.

But then the laughing stopped.

The girls started waving at their father and he waved back at them, but the more he waved the more agitated they became. It was only then that he realised that the girls weren't waving at him, they were warning him, what was happening behind him.

CRRRRRACCCCCCCKKKKKK!!!

Jonathan turned around at the loud sound, as the tree behind him, on the edge of the lawn, spilt in two vertically along the trunk. He turned back to the house to see his girls crying, as he tried to outrun the falling branches, as they seemed to reach out towards him with their spindly sharpened fingers.

Then within seconds, that seemed dragged out and much longer, one of the branches – all sharp and resembling a spear – bore down on him and then torn through his jeans, ripped through the soft flesh of his thigh and skewered him to the ground.

Screaming out loud as the searing pain went right through him, making him feel sick and almost pass out from the agony, Jonathan looked up at his daughters as they stayed in the window crying and still pointing.

The throbbing of his leg - as his jeans began to get soaked up with his blood - was unbearable and as he turned to look where the girls were pointing, the rain began to pour down on him as well.

A sudden crack of thunder and the rain unexpectedly became a torrential downpour. Lying in the mud, with his right leg pinned to the ground, Jonathan twisted his neck around to look behind him - to where the tree had fallen. Standing next to the shattered remnants of the tree was a man, with scruffy hair and blue overalls and he was laughing, loud and haphazardly and Jonathan could even hear his cackles over the rain and wind.

The man pointed at Jonathan and drew his finger across his throat in a cutting motion.

Jonathan stared at the man, through the waves of considerable pain that were flowing and emanating from his leg wound.

"WHO ARE YOU?" Jonathan screamed over the sound of the storm…

Nineteen

"I am Isaiah Clevedon and you shall feel my pain…"

Twenty

Moments later, Lisa came around the corner in their station wagon, just as the rain was easing off. The ground outside their home had turned to a 'mushy sludge' like brown chocolate soup and in the middle of the grass to the left of the driveway was Jonathan, impaled on the ground by a large 'spear-like' branch.

"Jesus..."

Turning off the engine, unclipping her seatbelt and diving out of the car, Lisa ran to Jonathan's side and looked at him - as he drifted in and out of consciousness. His leg was bleeding a little, but the branch was so tightly wedged that it was stemming the flow of blood seeping out; the branch was acting as a 'wooden plug' and certainly couldn't be removed.

"Darling what happened?" she said, beginning to sob, but trying to stay brave and rational – someone needed to be.

As his eyes opened he looked through the waves of pain and rain that was pouring down his face.

"I love you and I'm so sorry…"

"Sorry for what?"

"I'm, sorry that I brought us here, to this new home, to this island, for my new job…" he replied as he once more drifted out of consciousness, his eyes rolling up into his head, almost making him look like he was possessed.

As Lisa mopped his brow and rubbed the rain from his eyes, she started to cry even more. The tears flowed down her cheeks as she began to worry about the fact that she might lose her husband, like she'd almost lost her daughter from her fall. This house and the job, were gradually starting to look like an incredibly bad idea for their family and what had initially appeared to be the start of foundations for a new dream position for her husband and a great new beginning for their family, were rapidly turning sour and it was all revolving around past events that had occurred – and seemed to be still occurring - in and around the property.

"Mommie what's happening…?"

Lisa looked up from where she was sitting on the ground, to see both Kimmie and Sandra looming above her, the rain beginning to soak through their dresses, as they looked worriedly at their father, who appeared to be sleeping, still pinned to the ground.

"Get back in the house both of you and Kimmie, can you phone 911 and tell them that we have an emergency at Eden Lodge. Tell them that your father is losing blood and that he is in need of medical help."

****

Quickly Kimmie and Sandra ran to the house, the muddy slop on the ground splashing up on their legs, speckling them like freckles. Kimmie dragged her sister back through the front door and went to make the phone call.

Running into the hallway, Kimmie picked up the her Mother's cell phone, which was lying on the table next to the antique coat rack and quickly punched in the numbers 911, putting the phone up to her ear.

"Hello 911, which emergency please?" came the emergency telephone handlers reply.

"My Daddy has had an accident and he can't get up."

The operator then went through with Kimmie what the situation was.

'Was he hurt badly?'
'Was he bleeding?'
'Was her Daddy conscious?'
'Where was he currently?'
'Where did they live?'
'Was anyone else with them or were they alone?'

Kimmie answered all the questions as best as she could, all the while Sandra stood at her side, crying and listening to her sister talking; during this moment, Hycacinth and Emily stood at the top of the stairs, smiling and staring, no one able to see them as they were just far enough away to be out of view.

****

Sitting cross-legged in the pouring rain, Lisa mopped Jonathan's brow as she prayed for the soon arrival of the ambulance. She'd told Kimmie to say that he was losing blood, which was not really the truth as the branch was still wedged in and stopping any flow, but it would hopefully mean that the medics would arrive sooner, all flashing lights and a non-stop drive from the hospital to the property in as short a time span as possible.

As Jonathan looked at her - his eyes heavy from the pain and the shock that he was going through – he started to speak, the words coming out only as the faintest of whispers. Lisa leant forward, getting her ear close to Jonathan's lips so she could hear what he was trying to tell her, just as he said –

"There is something, in the woods…"

****

With a spinning of wheels and blue flashing lights, the ambulance and an accompanying police car arrived at Eden Lodge, sloshing through the mud and coming to a halt near the two figures on the grass.

Just off the driveway, they were still huddled together; husband and wife as one solid unit.

The rain had eased off and although soaked to the bone, they were both awake and alert as the emergency crews arrived. The 'spear-like' branch was still pinning Jonathan to the ground and Lisa was cradling his head in her lap, running her fingers through his hair in a calming motion, but still trying to keep him awake, talking to him constantly so that he was aware of what was happening.

The ambulance doors were thrown open and the two medics ran across the driveway and stopped beside Lisa and Jonathan, dropping to their knees and putting their bags down on the ground. The police who'd parked up behind the ambulance searched the perimeter of the property, looking for 'something'.

"Hello sir, can you hear me ok? What's your name?"

Lisa looked up and said, "he's my husband Jonathan, and he's the park ranger."

With that the two medics started to get to work on assessing the situation and what the best way forward was for their patient. They looked at the branch and realising that it was tightly wedged, they decided that the best plan of action was to take Jonathan back to the Hospital and see if they could fix him up there or if he would have to go back to the mainland.

The medics were called Scott Winslow and Dale Anderson and had both worked together, based at Martha's Vineyard Hospital, for the last three years - both having moved there from the mainland. They were both extremely experienced and skilled at their jobs and as Scott sat with Jonathan, checking his blood pressure and his temperature, Dale rushed back to the ambulance to grab a small electric handsaw.

Vital signs taken, Scott tried to see how attached Jonathan's leg was to the ground below and the answer was very solidly. Trying to move his leg a little, there was what looked like four inches of space between his thigh and the ground, enough space to work in, but it would need to be a very careful procedure, so that the branch wasn't displaced from the wound before they got back to the safety of the hospital and the plentiful supply of plasma, just in case he required a blood transfusion, when the branch was removed.

Dale came back from the ambulance, with the fully charged hand held electric saw. The saw was usually deployed for cutting through bones at the scenes of road accidents – of which there were few on the island - but this would be ideal to use in this situation, to cut the branch away from either side of Jonathan's leg and then to transport him from the driveway back to the hospital, for a further operation and the final removal of the remainder of the branch.

As Dale went through the details of what he was about to do with Jonathan and Lisa, Scott got a surgical knife out of his kitbag – the blade shimmering in the light – and cut through the material of Jonathan's trousers, to enable Dale to work his magic.

As the scene developed around her husband, Lisa watched over Scott's shoulder and saw Sherriff Dawson and Officer Martinez – weapons drawn – still carefully walking around the bushes and trees on the edge of their property. Eventually they stopped at the tree that had suffered the damage, where the branch that had speared her husband had come from. As they investigated the remainder of the branch, she could seem them talking to each other and looking at the trunk with extremely concerned looks on their faces.

Dale started up the electric saw and commenced cutting the branch underneath Jonathan, whilst Scott held the other half of the branch that was protruding from the front of his thigh. Lisa held her husbands hand as the cutting began, the blade flying through in no time at all, tiny splinters of wood and sawdust covering them all. As the branch was cut to a small stump protruding from the back of his thigh, Dale made a start on the front of his thigh and within a few short minutes Jonathan was no longer pinned to the ground and the two medics helped him to his feet and took him to the ambulance for his short trip to the hospital.

At that moment, the girls left the house and came to their mother, ready to go with her to the hospital, neither being old enough to be left on their own yet at their home.

As Jonathan was loaded into the back, Sherriff Dawson and Officer Martinez appeared at the side of the ambulance and intercepted Lisa as she attempted to follow her husband into the vehicle, with her girls, to look after her him on the short journey to the hospital.

"Hello again Mrs. Matthews, just a few questions to ask you before you leave" began the Sherriff, with Officer Martinez hovering behind him, looking extremely serious.

"Two things, one, were you here with your husband when this accident happened and two, did you see anyone else on your property?"

Lisa shook her head as she answered, looking confused at the questions.

"Jonathan was here on his own, the girls were in the house and I saw no one else here at all – why?"

Officer Martinez piped up before Dawson had a chance to answer Lisa's question, "the tree has axe marks on it, someone tried to chop it down, when the branches split – this might not have been an accident..."

Twenty-One

After the sheriff had finished talking with Lisa, she made her way into the back of the ambulance.

Both girls were crying and in a state of shock. Lisa hugged them and told them that everything was going to be okay, daddy just had an accident, and the paramedics will make him better. Sandra looked at her mother who was busy concentrating on what was happening with Jonathan;

"It wasn't an accident mommy, it was the bad man, he was in the backyard when the tree fell on daddy."

Lisa turned to her daughter and froze, the feeling of terror and dread dripped down her body like some grotesque disease. Lisa had to find out who exactly this Isaiah Clevedon was, to Lisa it was a matter of life and death now.

The journey to the hospital was swift, and Jonathan transferred into the acute care unit where doctors and a surgeon were already waiting for him. Lisa and the girls sat in the waiting room while the medical staff worked to save him. By now, Jonathan had been sedated and was pretty much out of it. Lisa and the girls could do nothing but wait until he was out of theatre.

A couple of hours went by, and the girls were getting restless, they had grown bored of the children's magazines that the hospital provided for bored kids in the waiting room, and they were starting to get hungry. Lisa sat the girls down.

"Right girls, I have something very important to ask you, and I want you to tell me as much as you know."

Both girls looked worried but were soon put at ease by their mother's soft-toned voice telling them everything was going to be ok.

"What do you want to know mommy?" Kimmie said in her usual but a slightly strained girlish voice, Lisa smiled at her and asked her what she knew about the bad man that was at the house. Kimmie lowered her head and thought about it for a few seconds before looking at Lisa and saying,

"He is a bad ghost mommy, he hurts kids, Hyacinth and Emily are scared of him too mommy."

Tears began to well up in Lisa's eyes, and she tried her hardest not to cry in front of her girls, she didn't want them worrying about her or the situation that was haunting them.

Lisa hugged Kimmie and told her not to worry that everything would be fine, the resilience in the two girls was astounding as they shrugged their shoulders and said

"Hyacinth and Emily are here to protect us, mommy, anyway they can..."

Lisa forced a smile before standing up to stretch her legs, worry still very much evident on her now tired anguished face.

****

After another couple of hours, both Lisa and the girls got escorted into a side room. Lisa feared the worst as the surgeon, Dr. Kowalski, a young good looking twenty-something man of Polish descent sat them down. After he had formally introduced himself as the surgeon who had operated on Jonathan, he gave Lisa the good news.

"Your husband was a very lucky man Mrs. Matthews, the piece of branch that pierced him clipped one of the main arteries in his leg, but because of the thickness of the branch, it miraculously blocked the immediate flow of blood. Your husband is going to be quite sore for a while, but I expect him to make a full recovery".

Lisa turned to her girls and with a smile said,

"See girls, daddy is going to be fine".

Both girls smiled back at her, their innocence firmly shaken but otherwise stable.

Lisa thanked the surgeon and asked if it was possible to see him. Dr. Kowalski said that he was still pretty much sedated and best to go home and come back in the morning when things were a little less chaotic, he should be pretty much awake by then.

After leaving the hospital, Lisa took the girls for something to eat, the time had dripped by quickly, and both girls were hungry, Lisa, not so much, she could do with something a little stronger, but knew she had to wait till she got back to the house. It was then she realised that she had no way of getting back to Eden lodge, as they had come via the ambulance.

It was only by sheer luck that Officer Martinez had come into the coffee shop for a beverage and seen Lisa and the girls sat down looking at her.

"Hello, Lisa, how is Jonathan doing?" Lisa smiled back at her and told her that he was going to be fine, it was then she kindly asked her for a ride back to the lodge.

"Sure," she said "come on I will take you back now."

The anxiety that coursed through Lisa's body seemed to dissipate, that was one less worry for her now.

Kimmie and Sandra finished their sandwiches and were quite happy sitting in the back of the police cruiser, while Lisa took the front passenger seat. Lisa and Officer Martinez kept the conversation to a minimum as they both could feel that the ordeal was only beginning, and for the sake of the two young girls in the back decided not to mention anything that had happened.

After Lisa and the girls were dropped off, she instructed both girls to go wash up and get their pyjamas, even with the chatter of the girl's voices and laughter, the house remained eerily quiet, as if the very brickwork itself was watching everything that was going on. The feeling of uneasiness loomed and made Lisa feel very uneasy but knew she had to find the strength, for her girl's sake. The past few days were weighing heavily on her mind. The ghost girls, Emily and Hyacinth, who by now Lisa was sure were real after getting the confirmation from the Haven Herald, but this Isaiah Clevedon, the thought of his mere name sent a sudden cold icy chill down her back. This scared her. She had to know who and what he was all about no matter how horrible a creature he turned out to be.

It was almost ten o'clock, and both girls had been asleep for a good hour or so, after the excitement of the day's antics, they succumbed to the tiredness.

Lisa poured herself a large glass of Black Bush whiskey, the stiffness as the cold amber liquid coursing down her throat made her almost gag, but it brought a bit of a relief to her. She didn't realise how emotionally drained she had become as the effects of the whiskey was sending her to sleep.

Lisa haphazardly made her way upstairs to her bed, each step of the stairs becoming more cumbersome than the last, and when she got to the last step, her ankles felt like lead weights.

Lisa checked on both girls one last time before heading off to sleep. It only took her five minutes, and Lisa was well on her way to dreamland. The house remained still, the sound of the clock in the kitchen echoed as the hands ticked on by into the small hours of the night.

****

Kimmie shifted in her bed, for some reason something or someone had awoken her from her sleep, or so she thought. She opened her eyes, her room belched in a blanket of darkness, and the only light she could see was from the two glowing eyes at the bottom of her bed. She closed her eyes again, and in that split moment she suddenly realised, somebody was there in the room with her. Kimmie's whole body froze with fright, she had been asleep, and it had taken a minute or two for her to wake up properly and register what was staring at her.

She couldn't move; she couldn't scream.

The smell of putrid flesh hung heavily in the blackness of her bedroom. Kimmie had tears streaming down her face as she felt the ghostly hand snatch at her bottoms. She was powerless. All she could do now is close her eyes and pray to God that he would make it stop, but he never heard her prayers.

Pain shot up through Kimmie's young body as if somebody was shoving a hot poker deep inside of her, yet still she was voiceless. Kimmie could now taste the stale stagnant breath of the bad man on her face, she wanted to gag, wanted to scream, wanted to run, but she couldn't. Kimmie had never in her life felt pain like this before. She was so scared; she could now feel the weight of the bad man pin her down on the bed, her arms and legs stretched out to the point of bursting out of their sockets. Kimmie closed her eyes and hid away in the recesses of her young mind in a bid to escape the horror that she found herself in. She finally drifted off into sleep.

****

The following morning Sandra had woken up early to go pee. As she made her way to the bathroom, she became aware of a faint whimpering. As she turned to face the staircase, she could see Hyacinth sitting with her knees up on the first step of the stairs. She looked at Sandra, and somehow subconsciously, her voice became loud in her mind.

"I'm sorry Sandra; we couldn't stop it; we couldn't stop it…"

With that Hyacinth turned her head and evaporated into the coldness of the morning air. It was now that an immense sense of grief and foreboding flooded Sandra's body, her legs felt like jelly, and she started to feel dizzy, pee soaked her pyjama bottoms and pooled around her feet. Something was wrong; something was very wrong.

The door to Kimmie's room was slightly ajar. Cold air seeped out from the gap and circled Sandra's legs, clinging onto her cold wet bottoms, Sandra shivered but edged her way slowly towards her sister's bedroom, she had never felt so scared and apprehensive in all her life. As Sandra pushed on the bedroom door, it creaked open, the sudden waft of something dead caused her to grip her nose to try and block out the smell. Her heart by now was thrumming like a guitar string. '

"Kimmie", Sandra called out but got no answer, she was hoping that she was still asleep, but somehow deep inside of her she knew that not to be the case. Sandra edged her way forward into her sister's room, the window was slightly open, and the curtains swished gently as the cold morning air swirled around the bottom of them.

"Kimmie", she called out again, and still nothing. A whimper came from behind her by the closet. Sandra quickly spun around to see Emily standing there, glaring over at the bed. Sandra was startled, but in her apprehension she plucked up the courage to talk to her ghostly friend.

"Emily, is my sister, ok".

Sandra's ghost friend turned her pale milk bottle face towards her. Translucent tears flowed from each eyeball, as she shook her head. Sandra still not fully aware of the gravity of the situation became scared. Kimmie wasn't answering or moving, so she crept back out of the bedroom and into her mother's room.

"Mommy, Mommy," Sandra stood at the side of the bed, shaking Lisa's shoulders in an attempt to wake her up. After a few moments, Lisa opened her eyes; she was still half asleep when she turned to see Sandra standing by her bed with a scared look on her face. Immediately Lisa shot up bolt straight in the bed. It was like somebody had just injected her with a full syringe of adrenaline.

"Sandra, What's the matter?"

Sandra turned to the bedroom door and just pointed in the direction of her sister's bedroom.

Lisa darted from the bed, almost bowling her youngest daughter over in the process. Now she could feel the oppressive atmosphere grabbing for her with unseen hands; she could sense the danger; she knew something was wrong.

Lisa quickly made her way into Kimmie's bedroom; the air inside was cold enough to take her breath away. Lisa ran towards the bed, she seemed to be sleeping, but she could see no movement of breath coming from her daughter.

"Good God no!"

Lisa's hands began to tremble as she pulled back the cover that draped over Kimmie. She screamed and fell to her knees. Kimmie lay on her side with her back towards her, her pyjama bottoms, torn and shredded from the leg to the crotch, and there was blood. Lots of blood.

Lisa grabbed Kimmie's shoulders and turned her over until she lay on her back. Her lips were ashen grey with a deep blue tinge and her mouth lay only partly closed. Congealed blood hung in clots from either side of her lips, and that is when Lisa noticed the two large open wounds meandering up from Kimmie's crotch and onto her stomach. Lisa had to steady herself as she looked down at the horror.

Carved into Kimmie's young stomach was the letters I.C. Blood had seeped out and dried as her body went cold.

Lisa screamed, "***YOU BASTARD***."

Twenty-Two

Outside the wind picked up. Dark gunmetal grey clouds gathered in a frenzy and threatened to release a torrent of rain on the dry land below. Inside Eden lodge, the air was thick, stagnant and hung down on its occupants like a chain around their necks. Within the confines of the shadows, Emily and Hyacinth hid out of sight. The evil that roamed inside the house was lurking, watching, waiting. It was only a matter of time.

Jonathan opened his eyes, somewhere in the vagueness, a voice was calling. The dim lighting of the ward made the floor almost look like amber. He was in pain and couldn't move. As he shifted his eyes back and forth to get some orientation of where he was and what had happened to him, the voice called his name again. Turning his head around either side of the bed, he was expecting to see a nurse or a doctor standing there, but nobody was.

Out of the corner of his eye, something moved towards him in the shadows, a black mass, skittled across the far wall and crept along the floor towards him. A sense of foreboding and uselessness crept up on Jonathan. Unable to take his eyes off the approaching darkness, Jonathan's mind exploded into a symphony of screams and wails. But something seemed familiar, too familiar to him, the screams, the cries, it was Kimmie.

She was in terrible trouble.

And then, the how, what, and why, was soon to make its presence known, but Jonathan already knew his name. Little did he realise, that it was already too late for his daughter, whatever the fuck this malevolent sonofabitch was, it had already struck. Darkness surrounded him once more.

As he lay drifting on the plains of netherness, Jonathan found himself floating above the woods. A sense of euphoria had guided him high above the redwood and sequoia trees, and he glided gracefully like that of an eagle.

Within the far right-hand boundaries of the forest, he spied a clearing, a mound of earth rose like a muddy pimple on the ground, and something sticking out from the dirt, something round, unable to quite see what it was, Jonathan willed himself down to take a closer look. The wheels of an old van protruded out from the earth. Its rust, flaking and broken off in chunks, had been buried sometime beforehand.

But why?

As he guided himself closer and closer to the clearing, a rush of wind lifted him back up higher past the outstretched grasping hands of the trees. Higher and higher he soared until he felt the subzero temperatures of the atmosphere stinging on his half-covered body. Jonathan closed his eyes once more.

He was back in the hospital, back on the ward. Warm air was surrounding him now, and he could sense the shapes of lights flicker past his closed eyelids. Jonathan opened his eyes just as two ghostly shapes dissipated into the fragments of the morning's early glow.

'*Shit*' he said to himself, as he lay confined to the hospital bed. '*Was it a fucking nightmare?*' Jonathan was still feeling a little groggy as the last of the sedation began to wear off him. Pain filled his body from the operation, and it hurt whenever he shifted in the bed. The events of the previous day came flooding back to him, and his mind was awash with so many unanswered questions.

Twenty-Three

The following three weeks were a living nightmare.

Kimmie had been gone for what seemed like a lifetime and Jonathan and Lisa both missed her like crazy, but no one missed the oldest child of the Matthews family more than her younger sister Sandra.

She cried herself to sleep every night, as did her parents, but they had each other for comfort in their bed, Sandra slept sobbing in her own bed alone.

The local police had put the murder of Kimmie down to a random intruder. A break in gone wrong, but even they both knew better, as did Jonathan and Lisa – it was something, in the woods and now it had 'attached' itself to their house and it had a name –

Isaiah Clevedon…

Twenty-Four

The funeral had been a small affair.

Due to Kimmie being so young and not attending school since the Matthews family had moved to Martha's Vineyard, there were no school friends, no teachers or members of the Board of Governor's.

A representative from the Eden Forestry Project had attended to support their employee at their time of grief, even though Jonathan didn't know who they were – a 'faceless suit' from his company's head office, just attending to show some kind of compassion, even though neither of them had ever set eyes on each other before and only exchanged the briefest of pleasantries.

Both Sherriff Dawson and Officer Martinez acted for the local Police department – both having met and dealt with Kimmie before, at what were now becoming regular events that were taking place at Eden Lodge.

And Ronnie Rydall from the Haven Herald was also in attendance. As she stood listening to the service, her feet shuffling slowly in the grass, her head down in shock, it was easy to see from her actions that she was finding it difficult to make eye contact with Kimmie's parents at the graveside – but it was obvious to anyone who cared to notice, that she wanted to.

The priest said a sombre blessing at the side of the open grave. When he finished, both Jonathan and Lisa moved forward and threw a handful each of dry earth down onto the tiny white, wooden casket, the final resting place of their oldest child. Jonathan allowed Lisa to throw her handful of earth in first as he leant on his stick, which he had been given on release from hospital – he was still walking with a noticeable limp, but able to walk at least and improving a little each day.

Sandra then came forward with a single red rose and a drawing that she had done of their family, so that she would never be alone and threw them down onto the coffin as well, sobbing all the time as she held her mom's hand.

Within another ten very long minutes, the funeral was over and they all began their procession of tears back to their transport, to take to the short drive back to their homes and work.

As the Matthews family neared their vehicle, Ronnie Rydall caught up with them and took Lisa to one side to have a quiet word with her.

"We need to talk. It just doesn't seem right that you have to endure all of this pain on your own. You have your family, but I know more about this situation than you might believe. Much, much more"

Lisa looked at Ronnie, unsure what she meant, still in shock from the recent events and everything almost seeming like a dream, a dense nightmare filled dream.

She hadn't been sleeping.

She had been to the doctor and he had dosed her up with Citalopram - anti-depressant pills – so every day was like a never-ending dream, with no light at the end of the tunnel. She had thought at her worst point about ending it all – but then what about Jonathan and Sandra? They certainly needed her, but what kind of help was she to them at the moment? None at all. She was vague, she was 'spaced out' and she was in another world, a world filled with thoughts and memories of Kimmie and bad images of that person – Isaiah Clevedon.

"Mrs Matthews? Can I speak to you at some point soon?" asked Ronnie, her eyes pleading with Lisa, as she absentmindedly looked back at her.

Half cracking a smile - as if to say thank you for being concerned – Lisa nodded her head in agreement.

"I'd like that" she replied. The thought of any company outside of the family might be just the kind of thing that she needed to try and get her to snap out of this 'funk' and come back as a person of use to her husband and daughter once more.

"Here's my number," said Ronnie, passing Lisa her business card.

Lisa flipped it over in her hand. On one side it had a colourful, small detailed map of Martha's Vineyard and on the other '***Ronnie Rydall – Receptionist***' in bold black print with the slogan '***Keeping Local News Relevant since 1949***' and her phone number below in clear embossed print; these were obviously quality business cards, Lisa thought as she placed the card inside her jacket and smiled back at Ronnie.

"I'll call you within the week, I promise."

With that Lisa turned her back on Ronnie, climbed into their car and Jonathan started the car up and they left the cemetery, Sandra in the back of the car, still looking lost, staring out of the rear window.

****

"Ring Ring Ring, Ring Ring Ring..."

The phone on the front desk of the Haven Herald rang and within seconds was answered by Ronnie, leaning across her desk, spilling the last of her morning coffee all over the day's paper in the process.

"Good morning, you're through to the Haven Herald, keeping local news relevant – how may I help you?"

The line went silent for a few seconds and then Ronnie heard a voice that she recognised on the other end of the line.

"I'm ready to talk with you..."

Twenty-Five

The doorbell rang at the Matthews home.

Lisa had already spotted the car coming up the driveway at a leisurely pace, as she was sitting with Sandra at the kitchen table; her daughter drawing and colouring as usual and Sandra staring into space, still in a daily state of hypnosis, a dream like state most of the time.

The home schooling had been put on the backburner and she was just spending her days sitting and wishing that she had been able to stop the torture that Kimmie must have gone through.

How could they have let such an awful thing happen to their beautiful little girl. Their little girl who had such a life ahead of her. Their little girl who was now only with them in their memories and photos. Their little girl who had been murdered by some filthy pervert, a grubby crank called Isaiah Clevedon.

Sleeping at night was difficult, truth be told extremely difficult. Short naps in the day were still interrupted by fleeting images of the person that she had seen reflected in the bedroom mirror and had come face to face with her in the bathroom as well. The lack of sleep was dragging her down and the skin under her eyes was sagging plus the lack of make-up made her look less 'fresh' and had aged her by years over a few short weeks – she'd looked at herself in the bathroom mirror that day and the woman that looked back at her had resembled her mother, more than the energetic faced 'home-schooler' that had smiled back at her every morning when Jonathan had taken up his 'dream job'.

But she had to be strong, she had to be 'motherly' to Sandra, as she was her sole focus now and she needed to make her life as happy a one as she could.

Also, Jonathan needed her help and support, as he was still off on sick leave from work, but his leg - and the pain when walking - was getting a little better day by day, even though on this day he was still asleep in bed, after a restless and painful sleep the previous night.

Snapping herself out of her current 'mood', Lisa ruffled Sandra's hair as she walked past her and across the kitchen floor, heading towards the front door and the bell that was still chiming, breaking the silence and making her more alert.

She got to the door and slowly opened it; the security chain was still on, everything made her nervous at the moment, with good reason.

The light from outside glinted on the chain as she open the door a crack and saw the light reflected in the squinting eyes of Ronnie Rydall as she looked through the gap at Lisa, all concerned smiles with an underlying look of worry in her well travelled face.

Ronnie was again wearing an ill-fitting top, her breasts trying to escape through the gaping chasms between the straining buttons.

As she smiled, her teeth sparkled in the reflection of the security chain, as Lisa pulled the chain back, opening the door wide and welcoming Ronnie in.

"I hope it's getting easier for you all?" she said, as Lisa directed her to the lounge, where they could have a chat on their own, in relative peace and quiet. As soon as Ronnie had said the line, she felt awkward – '*what can you say to a mother who's lost her child, without the comment sounding pointless…?*'

Lisa just smiled in reply – any answer seemed meaningless.

"I need to talk to you about what happened and the history behind it all."

Lisa sat down on the sofa, inviting Ronnie to sit in one of the floral print armchairs that were set up opposite her. The suite was extremely soft and comfortable and as Ronnie lowered herself onto the chair she sank into the cushions, like the chair had enveloped her, with material arms.

"I've brought with me the article that I didn't print out for you at the Herald. It's quite damning and it'll explain a lot…"

Lisa sat forward on the sofa as Ronnie leant in toward her, passing her a photocopy of a front page of the Haven Herald from fifteen years before, virtually to the day. Lisa held the paper in her hands as she settled back to read the details.

"Local Suspect Missing in Murder Enquiry"

"The prime suspect in the case of murdered child Mary McClellan, has gone missing, since being interviewed by the local police department on Martha's Vineyard.
Local D.I.Y. enthusiast Isaiah Clevedon was interrogated in depth at the local police station by Sherriff Jeremiah Dawson, who released the man on $10,000 bail, after a two-hour session with himself and his deputy.
All paperwork for the case has subsequently been passed to the District Attorney's office for decision and deliberation, over the evidence available with a view to possibly prosecute in this case.
Clevedon has since gone missing and the local police will be performing a 'door to door' investigation for further enquiries and to see if the local population have any verified siting's of this man.
Clevedon has previously spent time in South Bay House of Correction, being one of the first inmates transferred there on Boxing Day in 1991 when it opened – having been transported from the New Jersey area.
Mr Clevedon's lawyer Logan Williams has claimed that although his client is on bail and has a previous criminal record, he is not a danger to local residents and is now a reformed character of good repute, since his release from South Bay.
If the suspect is spotted anywhere on the island, please contact the Local Police force immediately."

Lisa sat back, unsure about what she had just read. The articles that Ronnie had provided her with before she'd not had the chance to read, as her husbands accident and life in general had already gotten in the way.

"OK, what do you think this means? Was he ever found and if not, how do we know that he was guilty? Innocent until proven guilty and all that. Right?"

Ronnie leant forward, her cleavage mesmerising Lisa as she began to speak.

"He was found…"

"Was he ever brought to trial and was he sentenced or found guilty?"

Ronnie wiped a tear from her eye as she reached out to hold Lisa's hand. Her fingers were smooth, her nails meticulously manicured, but her hands were clammy and damp.

"He was missing in the area for three days. He was eventually found near your property. He'd made a temporary bivouac and was living like a hobo - grubby, dirty and unclean. Eating road-kill and drinking fresh water from the river."

Lisa listened intently as she watched Ronnie recall the events of the days since he had gone missing and how he had been found in the woods.

"But was he guilty?" Lisa asked, her eyes pleading for some kind of resolution from the woman with all the answers.

"Oh yes, he was guilty, so, so guilty."

"But how do you know that he was guilty of anything? You must have been just a child at the time?"

"I know, all too well."

And with that Ronnie rose from the chair, standing up straight and grabbing hold of her belt that was holding her trousers up. She undid the belt, pulling the leather panel back through the buckle, loosening her trousers in the process. Her fingers clasped around the top of her zip as she dragged the slider down to the bottom stop, letting her jeans dropped to her ankles.

Her crisp white lacy panties, shone bright against her tanned skin as she walked closed to Lisa, who then noticed the marks on her legs.

Lisa looked at Ronnie's thighs and saw what looked like very old scars, but what must have been incredibly bad scars at the time. Running down the length of the inside of her thighs, were what looked like claw marks, like she'd been attacked by a wild animal. The gouges and scratches were deep and many and as she moved closer to Lisa she spoke.

"He came by our house in the night, when my parents were sound asleep."

As she got closer to Lisa, the penny dropped.

Lisa looked at the scars at the top of her thighs, near to her groin and there she saw what Ronnie was trying to relate to her.

Close in to her groin, amongst the 'long scratchy marks' were deep gouges and these scars were actually initials – once again the intials, just like Kimmie had been left with on her little body.

I.C. was carved deep and bold, near to her most private of areas.

Twenty-Six

Ronnie Rydall was only six years old when she first encountered the now deceased Isaiah Clevedon. It was the fall of '01, and the weather was threatening rainfall, with its dark grey monotonous clouds that blanketed the sun's chilling rays. Jennifer Rydall was dropping her youngest daughter off at the bus stop so that she could catch the school bus as it drove past. This was something that Jennifer had done countless times before, as it is a very small tight-knit community, the dangers of leaving her six-year-old at the bus stop were little to none, besides young Ronnie always buddied up with Alishia Cosgrove, a child that was two years her elder, who took it upon herself to mother Ronnie until they were safely on the bus and on their way to school.

At 08.50 am, the school bus turned up on time, as it did every morning. Both girls were busy chatting about the latest 'Scooby Doo' cartoon that was shown on television the previous night when the doors to the bus opened up. The bus driver, a middle-aged man, known to the girls as Mr Clevedon, had only been on the job a few months, he had taken over the responsibility of driver after Yolanda Barrett, the previous bus driver, who had suffered a massive stroke, and ended up paralysed all down her left side. Mr Clevedon was only too happy to take up the role as driver. He had been making ends meet in the town by repairing furniture, a small bit of mechanics and any other odd job that came his way. Mr Clevedon (Isaiah) had lived in the town all his life, and although considered a little odd and a bit of a loner, the residents of the town saw him as harmless and a perfect replacement for Yolanda.

The doors to the bus opened, and both girls got on. Ronnie smiled at the driver and said good morning as she tottled off to find a seat. Isaiah, looked in the rear-view mirror as the innocent six-year-old made her way down the aisle of the bus. Deep inside of Isaiah, something stirred a darkness that had been growing most of his life, a need that was slowly and methodically consuming him from the inside. He knew he had to have her. He would find a way.

Alisha saw things a little; differently, her being the slightly older of the two girls, always got a strange and uncomfortable feeling when it came to the new bus driver, it was a feeling of being watched, but what did she know, she was only eight years old. The bus took its usual route to school, stopping off along the way to pick up other children - it usually took about twenty minutes. Mr Clevedon always said have a good day to all the kids as they got off the bus. He watched as young Ronnie made her way into the school before pulling off to park the bus up.

Isaiah not only had the bus-driving job but was also tasked with stand-in janitor for Maurice Smyth whenever he had a holiday booked. It just so happened that Maurice Smyth had the last two days of the week off, as he had booked a long weekend break with his wife for their wedding anniversary. Isaiah made his way past the gymnasium and into the locked shed adjacent to the far end of the school. It was here all the mops, buckets and cleaning equipment along with various cleaning fluids and other hazardous materials - deemed too dangerous if got into the wrong hands - were kept.

Isaiah unlocked the huge padlock to the shed and made his way inside. His overalls hung on the hook just past the lockers used by Maurice and himself. School regulations stated that all personnel and workers within the school must have identification on display, but seeing as Isaiah only worked a couple of weeks of the year, he had his initials embroidered onto the pocket. It was good enough for him, and the school didn't take much notice as he was only there occasionally.

Isaiah pulled the overalls up over his faded, dirty blue denim jeans and was preparing to start the cleaning, once the initial school bell had gone off. He grabbed what equipment he needed and made his way over towards the side doors to the school. The wheels of the wheelie bucket creaked as he pulled it along by the handle of the mop that was sticking out.

"Damn shitty wheels" he mumbled to himself.

He made his way down the corridor towards the girl's toilets, (he always started there in case he got lucky to spy on any young unsuspecting students), an art that he was quickly mastering. Isaiah entered the girl's bathroom with his mop and bucket. He was supposed to put the yellow sign outside saying cleaning in progress, but he never did, *'why would he? and spoil his fun?'* He pushed open the doors to the four cubicles to make sure that they were indeed empty and began emptying the bins. Now and then he came across a used tampon or a pad from one of the older girls, this aroused Isaiah and made him want to masturbate.

After he had finished in the girl's bathroom, he made his way out to the corridor and began mopping up the corridors; chewing gum, candy and various other shitty stains from the herds of dirty trainers mosaicked the red-tiled flooring. It was a job that he hated doing, and under a tirade of fucks and dirty bastards, he grumbled to himself. The school itself had a pupil range from early years, i.e., from the age of five upwards to thirteen, as it was only a smallish town, it catered for a variety of kids, including special needs children. It comprised of Autistic, Cerebral Palsy and Downs children. Isaiah glanced up as he heard the door opening. Marcie Billings, a young nine-year-old with the mental age of five, was making her way out to use the bathroom. He watched as the young girl skipped on by him, smiling. Something inside of Isaiah stirred and with a glance around to ensure the corridor was deserted, he followed the young girl inside.

Isaiah dropped the yellow cleaning sign outside the bathroom and closed the door. He could hear Marcie still singing to herself as he quietly made his way inside. She was in the 2nd cubicle, and the door was only closed over and not locked. Isaiah felt the aching in his groin as he shuffled closer and closer to the unlocked door. Beads of sweat dripped down his forehead as he anticipated what he was going to do next.

Marcie felt the hand go over her mouth from behind. She stood up in the cubicle with her back to Isaiah. She struggled with fright at what was happening. Tears flowed down onto Isaiah's hand as the grip on her mouth became tighter and tighter. Marcie felt the prodding at her backside as the monster bent her forward. The fire within the eyes of Isaiah was wild and relentless. Marcie's body became limp, and she slumped forward onto the toilet. She was unconscious. Isaiah fumbled at the zipper to his overall's, desperate to get his penis out but then panicked. Outside he could hear talking. Isaiah froze. He knew he only had a small window of opportunity, which was quickly closing in on him. He had to get out of there; he mustn't get caught.

Isaiah waited for the chatter to become distant before he opened the door to the bathroom. He glanced outside quickly to be sure whoever it was, had gone and that it was safe for him to leave. Isaiah looked over his shoulder; he could still see the legs of the young girl poking out from under the toilet door. He grabbed the cleaning sign and hurried to the far end of the corridor. He had to act as normal as possible. After a few minutes, Isaiah could hear the squeak of the bathroom door opening; without looking back, he carried on mopping the floor, whistling the tune to 'The Great Escape'.

It made him laugh inside. He had just made his 'great escape'. After fuelling his need for young girls, his near sexual experience with Marcie Billings, only fed his hunger to try again.

Next time he wouldn't fail.

****

Marcie Billings opened her eyes. She was lying on the floor in the cubicle with her panties around her ankles. Confused and disoriented, she struggled to her feet, and still quite wobbly, she clumsily sat herself down on the toilet. She didn't know what had happened. After regaining a little more strength, she pulled her pants up and pulled the flush. Once she had washed her hands, Marcie left the bathroom. Up ahead she could see the janitor mopping the floor at the far end of the corridor, he was whistling and had his back to her. Without saying a word, she went back into her classroom and sat down, not knowing what had just happened to her, and how lucky she had been; she remained silent.

Twenty-Seven

Ronnie Rydall finished her class at 3 pm; she would wait by the entrance to the playground for Alisha who finished class ten minutes later than her, as she was that couple of years older. Ronnie stood by the doors as usual and watched as the other pupils left school for the day.

Isaiah Clevedon was in the janitors shed, his hand stroked the top of his penis through the dirty blue overalls, as he was still thinking about the incident earlier on in the day. By now, it was time to get out of the overalls and into his usual attire, school time was almost up. As he peeled the grubby clothing off himself and threw them into his holdall, they would come in handy for working on his van; he glanced out the window. Ronnie Rydall was stood by the double doors adjacent to the playground, with her pink Barbie rucksack, to Isaiah, she looked delicious. Suddenly, the sick inner voice began to speak to him.

"Isaiah, Isaiah, look at her, you know you want her, you know you have to have her, she wants you, she needs you, you can almost taste her sweetness".

Spit dribbled down the side of Isaiah's mouth as he stared through the dirty window of the shed at the little six-year-old. His inner voice was urging him to get her. Isaiah grinned as the voice inside gave him instructions.

"Call her over, she will come to you, she trusts you, smell her, she is waiting for you".

Isaiah opened the door to the shed and stood just outside. The majority of the pupils that were leaving at 3pm had already made their way to their parent's cars, which left only a handful of students loitering at the far end of the playground. Isaiah waved at Ronnie. Ronnie looked over to see who was waving at her. Mr Clevedon was calling her over, she thought about waiting for Alisha to come so they both could go, but he was an adult, and she could trust him. Ronnie smiled and trotted over towards the shed to see what Mr Clevedon wanted. The sun was threatening to burst through the overhead clouds as a slight breeze wafted down the playground.

"Hello Mr Clevedon", the little girl was smiling at the bus driver as he smiled back at her.

"Hello there little Ronnie, I guess you have finished for the day". Ronnie grinned and said in her angelic voice,

"I sure am Mr Clevedon."

"Please, call me Isaiah" he said to Ronnie.

She smiled and nodded in agreement. Isaiah had to get her in the shed.

"I've got something really fun to show you; it's just here by the lockers, it's a surprise".

Ronnie stood on her tippy toes and tried to see past the bus driver, but his shoulders were too broad and blocked her view.

"Erm, O.K Isaiah," she said as she slowly walked inside the dimly lit shed. Isaiah took one final look upon the playground before closing the shed door behind him.

Isaiah pushed the girl hard in the back; Ronnie flew forward, bouncing her head on the opened locker door. She shrieked as her face exploded in a burst of red as blood splattered across the inside of the locker. Ronnie began to cry as the terror took hold of her. The bus driver grabbed her again and slammed her head down on the floor.

"You're mine now bitch" he snarled, baring his yellow stained teeth.

[omitted] By now, Ronnie had passed out with the pain and lay motionless on the cold floor of the shed. [omitted]

From start to finish, the whole sordid process only took a matter of ten minutes. Ronnie lay curled up in the foetal position; blood started to congeal from the wound on her head, her eyes remained closed and a whimper, hardly audible to Isaiah's ears, escaped from her mouth, but he didn't care, he had his fun. Looking at his young victim, Isaiah grabbed a small parcel knife that was on the bottom of the locker. He knew that he had crossed the line and that he had to act fast, but the sickening voice inside his mind whispered to him once more. As Ronnie lay helpless, Isaiah carved his initials out on the top of her thighs. The inner voice laughed cruelly,

"Now she is yours forever".

Blood oozed out of the red angry looking letters. He just smiled at his handy work. It was the mark of a madman.

****

Aleisha was waiting by the doors for Ronnie; she was running slightly behind as the stupid teacher Ms Smale had made her pick up the rubbish that the boys had been throwing at each other. She couldn't see Ronnie anywhere. The school bus had driven into the playground and was waiting down by the gated entrance. Mr Clevedon was fifteen minutes late today, and the other students were growing impatient. The doors opened, and Aleisha made her way down the playground; still, she couldn't see Ronnie. Mr Clevedon sat watching the pupils get on board the bus, his face flushed, and his hair matted from sweat. A fresh red stain was visible on the leg of his dirty jeans. Aleisha, who by now was concerned for Ronnie asked Mr Clevedon to hold on for her. Isaiah's eyes fluttered as he looked away and said –

"Sorry kid, I'm already running late".

Aleisha sat down as the bus pulled off.

****

Sheriff Dawson parked up in the layby, just off route 21. It had been a slow day, and he was already feeling tired. Traffic at that time of day was quiet as most of the parents had already picked up their kids from the school. He switched on the radio and put it on low; it was mainly for background noise rather than the shitty tunes the station was currently playing.

Officer Martinez was back at the station catching up on the pile of paperwork that she was supposed to do earlier on in the week when she got the phone call. One of the locals was walking his dog just off route 19 when he came across a badly beaten young girl in the bushes. Brandi Martinez got straight on the blower to Sheriff Dawson, who instructed her to meet him at the location.

****

With his blue lights flashing, Jeremiah Dawson screamed his cruiser down the road towards route 19. It was a ten-minute drive, but at that speed, he made it in just under six.

The ambulance was already on the scene as he pulled up alongside. The young girl was already on the gurney as the paramedics were working on her. Bill walked towards them. Looking at the young victim, who was alive, but only just, his heart sank as the paramedics took the oxygen mask off to insert a tube down into her stomach.

"Oh, my good God, No".

It was Ronnie, Jeremiah's six-year-old niece. She had been raped and beaten, but she was alive. Sheriff Dawson fell to his knees, and with his head, in his hands, he cried.

Once in the hospital, the extent of Ronnie Rydall's injuries became apparent. Whoever had done this to her was one sick individual.

Twenty-Eight

As time went on, Ronnie Rydall made a slow but almost full recovery. She spent almost two months in hospital and countless hours with a therapist, to try and come to terms with her ordeal. Ronnie wouldn't speak of her attack, each time, when questioned about what had happened, she started to shake uncontrollably, go all clammy and shut down. The therapist said it was a coping mechanism. After a lengthy investigation, only one suspect fit the bill, but due to a lack of evidence, Isaiah Clevedon was a free man.

Sheriff Dawson and the townsfolk were outraged.

A deep-seated hatred spread among the people.

It was the 17th of February, five months since Ronnie Rydall was attacked, Mary Jenkins, A redheaded middle-aged woman of Irish descent and the wife of the local baker, stopped Sheriff Dawson as he headed towards the cafe for his morning coffee,

"Sheriff Dawson, may I have a word please", Bill Dawson turned to face Mary.

"Sure Mary, how is the bakery doing?"

Mary said "Good, but enough of the chit chat, we want to know what's happening about Clevedon?"

Bill took his hat off and rubbed his face with his free hand. "Listen, Mary, I understand completely that justice has failed, there is nobody more than myself that wants to see that Bastard off our streets", Mary cut Bill's conversation short,

"No, you don't understand Bill, if you don't do something about Isaiah Clevedon, then the rest of us will".

Bill shook his head in disagreement,

"Now Mary, don't be going doing anything foolish and fool hearty, his time will come, I promise you."

Mary Jenkins turned and started to walk away from the sheriff, but not before giving him one last piece of advice.

"If I were you, Bill, I would think long and hard exactly to whom your loyalties lay, the time is ticking".

****

Isaiah Clevedon got into his Volkswagen camper van and started down route 15; He wanted to get out of the town for a couple of hours, ever since his dealings with the local law, he had to keep things on the quiet. But it was a small community, word travels quick, way too quick.

The weather was pretty rough for this time of year, and a heavy depression hung around his neck like an iron noose. This sickness that was inside of him craved the taste of young blood again.

As he passed the small dirt track to Eden lodge, and down past the bridge, he noticed that a small car had broken down on the side of the road. Its occupants were stood outside with the hood of the car up. Isaiah pulled over to see if they needed any help.

Gretchin Lewis sat in her booster seat in the back of the car, she had just turned five a couple of days previously and eagerly watched as the man got out of the van and walked up to her parents, Briony and Jacob.

"Hello there," Isaiah said "do you need any help?"

Jacob looked across at his wife, who was busy fumbling about with her bag; he knew who Isaiah was and also knew the allegations against him. The sight of him standing there knowing what he had done made Bryony physically sick to her stomach. The weather was taking a turn for the worst, and the Lewis's knew that they would be screwed if caught out here in a storm. Jacob had already called for the pickup truck but knew it was going to be another hour or so before it got to them.

"No, we are fine, thank you", Jacob said.

Isaiah looked at the young kid in the back of the car.

"And who do we have here?" he waved at Gretchin and smiled at her.

Bryony screamed at him.

"Get away from her you sick bastard".

Isaiah froze as the woman frantically ran towards her daughter, who was now smiling back at him. Jacob, being the red-blooded male that he was, ran for Isaiah. His fist connected cleanly with his bottom lip, and Isaiah fell backwards and smashed the back of his head on the car's bumper. Pain shot through Isaiah's head as blood spilt out from the wound. He lay propped up against the front of the car. He tried to move his body to a standing position, but his body refused to move.

Isaiah was now panicking as his head became more and more heavier and he struggled to keep his eyes opened. He was fading fast.

Jacob phoned Jeremiah Dawson. Bill was in the coffee shop chatting to the waiter Benjamin Shields, they had grown up together and had remained friends when his phone went off.

"Hello Jeremiah, it's Jacob Lewis here, I need your assistance, I have broken down a half-mile past Eden lodge, something has happened, and I need you to come."

"What's happened Jacob? You sound all flustered."

His phone went silent for a couple of seconds before Jacob spoke again.

"I think I've killed that paedophile, Isaiah Clevedon".

Jeremiah's eyes widened as the words he had just heard hit him on the inside like a shotgun blast.

"I'm on my way," Jeremiah said.

Benjamin Shields watched as the sheriff got up and left abruptly. He had overheard the conversation that the sheriff just had and was only too happy to spread the word to the people that mattered.

****

Jeremiah Dawson rounded the bend fast just after the old bridge. It had been raining heavily on the way, which made the roads more treacherous, and he almost lost control as he braked hard. Jacob Lewis was standing next to his car on the grass verge waving at him. Sheriff Dawson pulled up just behind the Volkswagen and quickly made his way over to the Lewis's. The body of Isaiah Clevedon lay slumped by the front of the car, blood stained his shirt and pooled with the freshly dropped rain by his arms.

"Holy Shit, what the hell happened here?"

Briony was sat in the passenger seat comforting her daughter, wiping fresh tears from her face. Jacob began to explain to the Sheriff what had occurred a short time previously.

After Jacob had explained what had happened to the dead man lying in front of his car he turned to the Sheriff and asked what was going to happen to him.

"I don't want to go to prison over this Jeremiah; he is a pervert and, we all know he had it coming, I was protecting my daughter."

But Jeremiah Dawson couldn't justify the cause.

"Jacob, how long have we been friends?"

Jacob shook his head and replied, "about thirty years."

"Just look at the position you are putting me in, I am the Sheriff for fuck sake",

"I know that Jeremiah, but come on, nobody is going to miss him, you gotta help my family and me out".

Both men were interrupted by a truck, which was coming from the town. Its lights were on, and it was driving slowly. Jacob watched as the truck rounded the bend and pull up beside Sheriff Dawson's cruiser. It was Henry Morton, the proprietor of Morton's mechanics and breakdown services. A good friend of Jacob's, but he wasn't alone, he had two other people with him.

Henry and his two passengers stepped out and walked towards Jacob and the Sheriff.

"How do Jacob", Henry said as he stood there in a black parker jacket and woolly hat to match. His two passengers, Norman Jenkins, the baker and Simon Cortez, who owned the hardware store three doors away from the bakery.

"It's ok Jacob we know what's happened, Jeremiah what are we going to do about it?"

"How do you know what has happened?" Jeremiah said in an anxious voice.

"Your phone-call in the cafe, Ben Shields informed us of the situation, and we are here to help".

"Help with what?" Jeremiah said.

Henry looked at both Jacob and Jeremiah and said,

"Help with burying this fucker in the woods".

Jacob now felt a sickly feeling in his stomach as the whole gravity of the situation was starting to sink in.

"Come on Jeremiah; you can't let him go down for something that we all wanted to do, you know full well that Isaiah Clevedon is a rapist and paedophile, shit Jeremiah it was your own niece that suffered at the hands of him".

Jeremiah put his hand up, turned and strolled away from the small crowd. He had a decision to make, and he had to do it quickly. After a couple of minutes or so he walked back, his head was telling him to do the right thing and uphold the law, but his heart was telling him otherwise. He knew if he arrested Jacob for this that his life in the town would be unbearable, and his sister would never forgive him.

"Ok, how are we going to do this?"

After placing the road closed signs on both sides of the bridge, the five men set to work digging a hole big enough for the van. It was hard work, but with five of them on the job they soon got through it. Once they had finished burying the camper van with its owner inside, Sheriff Dawson turned to face Jacob and the other three men.

"Nobody must speak about this".

Everybody agreed to take the secret to their grave. Isaiah Clevedon was never seen alive again.

Twenty-Nine

"And that's how these scars came to be a reminder," explained Ronnie as she quickly pulled her trousers back up, tears cascading down her cheeks as she recalled the events to Lisa, who was sitting rocking to and fro, thinking about her daughter and how this person had endured a similar horrific attack.

Ronnie had been lucky to survive, Kimmie had not.

Out on the chilly breeze outside, a bird flew past the window, a crow – briefly looking in and seeing the two women in deep conversation and then moving on. A possible warning or ill omen, given the circumstances that were rapidly developing around the property.

"How do you get over something like this?" she asked, passing Ronnie a box of tissues to dry her face.

The tissues were a children's brand of the 'Scooby Doo' variety and one of Kimmie's favourites; there were reminders of the Matthews eldest daughter everywhere in the house, from the toys still scattered around, to the drawings and coloured in pictures displayed with Sandra's on the refrigerator – she would never be forgotten.

As Ronnie took a tissue and began to carefully dab at her eyes, trying not to smudge the majority of her make-up, she looked at Lisa and shrugged, her breasts shifting with the movement, again trying to escape her blouse.

"Life goes on. You just have to put all the dreams and nightmares into the past, make them seem like they weren't real and then it becomes slightly easier to come to terms with them, but it's still not easy. As the days turn to weeks and then into months and years, what actually happened begins to seem like a bad memory, but you truly never forget it, deep down that feeling is always there, buried deep down in your psyche, causing an ill feeling in your gut, when something triggers the 'bad thoughts'. It still chills me to the bone to think about it and the dreams still come to me at times, especially when I am feeling down or low. But I have moved on and most of the time I am fine."

Lisa nodded, trying to smile, but finding it more difficult than she would have weeks ago.

It wasn't easy listening to this, it was even more problematic thinking that she and Jonathan had been in the house, but had heard nothing. If they had heard a scream or even a whimper they might have been able to save her, but she must've been scared rigid, unable to call for help, unable to cry for her parents - her loving mom and dad who were only a few steps away down the corridor.

"Where do we go from here?"

Lisa looked at Ronnie.

Ronnie smiled back at her.

"We can try to get on with our lives and make these events a thing of the past, best forgotten or we can try and do something about it and put an end to this evil nonsense forever."

Ronnie ran her fingers up and down the seams of her jeans, thinking about what she'd just said. How could they do something about it?

Isaiah Clevedon was dead.

He wasn't coming back, but his 'evilness' was emanating everywhere in the property and even though it was a bright and sunny day, the house felt dark - like a blanket of malevolence was enveloping the whole house and dragging the family's lives down with it. Ronnie looked around at the room, thinking that she saw a fleeting glance of a child in the doorway, but in a brief fraction of a second the image was gone – did she see something or was it just the house playing tricks on her?

She moved her concentration back to the job at hand and looked Lisa in the eyes; she would need to be a support and a rock for her 'new friend' and provide the support that people had given her when she'd been that confused and hurt child, all those years ago.

"I think that we need to speak to someone and when I say 'we', I mean you and I. If we were to pay a visit with your husband as well, it might not help as this person is in a fairly fragile state of mind and bringing another male into his currently unstable environment might not help him or us."

Lisa looked at Ronnie and Ronnie leant forward to touch her hand.

"I think that we need to go and see the previous Forest Manager for Eden Projects – we need to pay a visit to Jeffrey Walsh."

Thirty

Hours later Lisa tucked Sandra in to her bed and put the night light on, displaying star maps all across the ceiling of her bedroom. She was sleeping much better now, but still felt comforted by the additional glow in her room.

As she left through the door, she heard a little voice call her from her bed.

"Mommy, do you think that Kimmie is still here with us?"

Lisa turned on her heel and went back in to her daughter's room.

"I'm sure she will always be with us in our hearts darling," Lisa replied as she went over and sat down on Sandra's bed.

Sandra sat up in bed and kissed her mom on the cheek.

"Hyacinth and Emily said that she's here now and she plays with them all the time."

Sitting up straight, Lisa looked at her daughter as she lay back down on her pillow and the tears began to well up once more in her eyes. She seemed to spend a great deal of the time crying at the moment, which was expected, given the situation that they were all still going through; even the usual day to day chores were hard work and every time she went into Kimmie's room, she still expected to see her come running to her.

"What have they said to you?"

Sandra lifted her head up off the pillow and reached out to hug her mom.

"They both told me that she is very happy – most of the time – and they are with her a lot here in the house, but that nasty man is also here at times as well."

'Isaiah Clevedon, will he ever leave us alone?' Lisa thought to herself as she ruffled and tousled her daughter's hair with her left hand.

"Darling, go to sleep now and dream of nice things, what you want for Christmas and what we'll do with the tree this year." Christmas was still months away, but it might take her mind off 'spirits' enough for her to be able to get to sleep.

Lisa then stood up and went out the door. Her daughter was almost asleep before she pulled the door shut, until just a crack was open, so that she could hear anything if she became disturbed in the night.

She walked along the hallway and went into her bedroom.

Jonathan was in bed already - where he'd been most of the day – watching the end of a movie and chuckling away to himself, trying to cheer himself up. Since the 'event' Jonathan had really taken it badly. Despite the pain that he had been in from the tree branch, he was still able to sleep and that was what he was doing most of the time.

Dosed up with a combination of Fentanyl for the pain and Prozac for the depression, Jonathan was drifting in and out of sleep, waking for the pills and a little to eat – usually not enough, especially compared to what he would be normally eating when he was working. His work was really physical, but at the moment there was no way that he would be able to return to it or in the near future, but he still talked about his job everyday, wishing away the pain and the 'low mood' that was enveloping him.

Lisa slipped out of her trousers and top, peeled off her underwear and dragged on her slouchy pyjamas – climbing into bed next to Jonathan, plumping up her pillows, just before she lay down.

"I absolutely love The Three Amigos," slurred Jonathan, a combination of the pills and being on the edge of sleep now kicking in. As Steve Martin, Chevy Chase and Martin Short were summoning the 'Invisible Swordsman', Jonathan drifted off to sleep and Lisa flipped the TV back on to stand-by, turning the lights off and shutting her eyes.

As Lisa gradually went to sleep, all she could think of was Isaiah Clevedon, Jeffrey Walsh and the possible closure for the whole horrid situation that she and her family were currently still in and living through day to day.

****

Three days later the phone in the hallway rang and Lisa jogged in from the garden to answer it.

"I've managed to pull a few strings and we have a meeting with Jeffrey Walsh at his care home. It's a secure unit, some of the patients - Jeffrey included – are locked away in their rooms most of the day; they're not usually allowed out on their own unsupervised due to their fragile mental state, but Jeffrey has caused no problems in the time he's been there, so we have been granted a meeting with just him and us. It could be a very interesting visit."

"Ok, when are we going?" Asked Lisa, tapping her fingers nervously on the telephone table.

"Tomorrow morning at 10:30am, they've given us an hour with him, which should be plenty of time."

What could possibly go wrong, Lisa thought to herself as she said her goodbyes to Ronnie and hung up the phone.

It would be good to speak to Jeffrey Walsh, someone who had been through a similar situation to them. It was a little worrying that he was now in a guarded facility, but perhaps he didn't have the support of a good family or he was just a little unstable to start with?

The following day would provide the answers and Lisa was ready to embrace them and hopefully help her and Jeffrey's situations in the process.

****

With a beep of her horn, Ronnie's SUV drove up the driveway and parked up by the front door of the Matthews home. The sun was shining and for the time of year it was quite a nice day. Winding down the window and waving to Lisa as she closed the front door, Ronnie looked completely un-phased by the situation; though she still bore the scars of her encounter, they were a long time ago and she had compartmentalised that part of her life deep at the back of her mind - best forgotten, best not thought about.

As Lisa climbed in the door, Ronnie turned to her.

"Are you ready for this then?" She asked, sensing the tense feelings already in the car - even her memories would be coming back today, when they started talking about 'him'.

"I guess we both have to be - let's get this shit over with."

With that Ronnie spun the car around - pebbles and tiny stones being spat out from under the wheels as she headed back down the driveway and off in the direction of their destination.

Twenty minutes later and several tracks from Joan Jett's greatest hits album and they turned into the approach to Waverley House, the care facility where Jeffrey Walsh was currently a long term resident - with no indication that he would be released in the near future.

Ronnie explained to Lisa before they left the car that she had spoken about the proposed visit to the Senior Care Officer Sam Wells, who she knew from a previous article that had been written by the Haven Herald. When the article had been published in the paper, it had praised the establishment so much for its high standard of duty of care to the patients, that Sam had popped into reception to pass on a letter from the owner Edward Silverstein thanking their paper for it's complimentary coverage and providing free passes to their 'Summer Jamboree' fundraiser that year, providing the Herald with free food and drink all day.

Ronnie had attended with several other members of staff and they'd all had a great time.

The patients were all kept in their rooms for the duration of the event, but when the band that played, paused between songs, some could be heard hurling abuse and crying from their rooms across the field.

Ronnie had spent a good hour chatting to Sam, as they'd found out that they both had a strong passion for Boston Celtics and each had a deep admiration of Larry Bird - their one time small forward/power forward and receiver of the NBA MVP three times in the '80s. Through this mutual admiration they'd kept in touch and even attended a couple of games together in Boston, but nothing more than that, neither were interested in a relationship or anything sexual and were just content to be 'good friends'.

So, when she had rang Sam to ask if they could have a word with one of their patients - Jeffrey Walsh - he had agreed readily and given them an hour slot, not even querying what it was for, he trusted Ronnie that much and assumed it was for the paper.

Getting out of the car, they both walked around to the front and stood looking at the building - Waverley House.

It was an imposing building. A white monolithic structure that was characterless, but full to the brim with characters, most of them dosed up to the eyeballs on sedatives such as Methaqualone or Quaaludes - as they used to be known by.

"Let's go then," said Ronnie as she guided Lisa by the arm up the steep stone steps and in through the main doors of the facility.

Inside the main reception area everything was clinical, as you'd expect from a medical care centre, but it was whiter than white and almost made you want to wear sunglasses indoors due to the intense glare from all the reflecting light on the walls.

As they walked up to the reception - manned by a stern looking woman, late 50's, jet black hair and a mole the size of a gobstopper on the left side of her temple, Ronnie moved forward and said -

"We're here to visit one of your residents, Jeffrey Walsh, we are expected"

As the receptionist looked on the screen diary to check for their appointment, a shout came out from behind them.

"GO CELTICS!!!!"

Ronnie and Lisa spun around to see a tall man, dark hair, late 40's, carrying a lot of weight, looking 'solid', in a white uniform, coming bounding down the hall to greet them.

"Hi Sam" hollered Ronnie as the man - who was the size of a bear - picked her up and appropriately gave her a huge bear hug.

"How are things going then? Is this your friend Lisa that you've told me about?"

Lisa gave a small wave and a half-hearted curtsy as Sam strongly shook her hand.

"You've got to be strong to work here" said Sam, having noticed her slight wince - he did sometimes apply too much pressure when greeting people at the facility and he had to remember to be slightly less 'vigorous' especially when meeting female visitors for the first time, sometimes male strangers didn't take it so well either.

"If I escort you both down to Meeting Room 5, I'll bring Jeffrey in for a chat. He hasn't had any visitors in a long while, so I'm sure he'll be very talkative. He's not been a problem since he's been here either, so you can have the visit unguarded if you want? He'll not be any trouble, never has been, never is."

With that they were checked through the security doors and Sam talked to Ronnie about how the current Celtics season was going, as they walked along the corridor and up the first lot of steps.

Everywhere looked unbelievably clean, clean enough to eat your food off the floor, if you were so inclined - and some of the residents were.

As they took a left at the top of the staircase, the windows on the right hand side of the corridor looked out across the gardens and grounds of the property. There were about a dozen patients out there enjoying the sunshine, some walking around with orderlies, some sitting, some standing and one naked old woman running around and being chased by two members of staff.

"That's June, she does that all the time. She used to be a naturist in her younger years, now she's 74 and she still pulls all her clothes off at any chance she gets. It can be a little unnerving for the other patients, but we have to put up with these things, she suffered a brain injury and it affects all her rationality- she's always 'locked away' when we have the 'Summer Jamboree's', we wouldn't like her upsetting any of the local businessmen!!! Plus we found her in the bushes once with one of the other 'older patients' - but the less said about that the better!"

They then went up another flight of steps and passed through another security door, Sam keying in his personal number and putting his hand on the reader to scan his fingerprints. The door opened and they were on a direct replica of the floor below and Lisa could see June, now being manhandled under a blanket towards the entrance, back into the facility from the garden - her fun was over for the day.

Walking on down the corridor, they stopped outside a room with a large number 5 above the door in bright red acrylic - Meeting Room 5.

"OK, if you both want to mosey on in and take a seat, I'll go and collect your interviewee from his room, he's been awake and waiting for you for hours."

Ronnie and Lisa walked into the room. It was again 'whiter than white' and consisted of a large rectangular oak table, the kind that was thick and very heavy and four equally heavy leather armchairs, two on either side facing each other, almost like they were set up for a job interview, a very comfortable and relaxed job interview.

Ronnie sat down first, as Lisa looked around the room, getting her bearings. There were no windows looking into or out of the room, there was only a huge frosted skylight, which flooded the room with bright sunlight, making it seem like it was almost like being outside, indoors.

There were a couple of limited edition prints on the walls, screwed on there, so that they couldn't be removed and used as a weapon.

Lisa then sat down next to Ronnie, looking at the disconcerting scratches and gouges scattered across the table top - some patients were obviously a little more agitated than others; hopefully their meeting would be less eventful.

The door then opened and Sam ushered in a man in a loose fitting t-shirt and jeans. He appeared to be in his late 40's, his hair was cropped short and he had a bewildered look when he shuffled into the room, but managed a smile as he saw the two women sat at the table.

His t-shirt bore the classic slogan 'Keep on Truckin'', with the print having almost worn out due to constant washing and drying.

"These are the two ladies that I was telling you about, they're both from the paper, the Haven Herald and they've come to interview you for it."

Lisa looked at Ronnie who quickly shook her head as she stood up and thrust out her hand.

"Hello, I'm Ronnie."

"Jeffrey" he replied looking a little shocked at the forwardness of Ronnie, as he turned to Lisa.

Lisa jumped up and shook his hand introducing herself and sitting back down.

Jeffrey then walked around to the other side of the table and squatted down in one of the leather chairs.

"I'll be back in an hour," said Sam as he walked out of the room, making sure that it was securely locked after him, giving Ronnie the 'thumbs up' through the glass pain down the centre of the door.

They both looked at Jeffrey.

Where were they to start?

Neither of them had been in a situation this awkward - how could they bring it up, in a way that didn't upset him? That didn't drag up the issue of Isaiah Clevedon again- the main reason that he was locked up in this institution in the first place.

"What do you know about Isaiah Clevedon" Lisa blurted out.

The mood in the room suddenly changed.

Jeffrey leant back in his chair, looking more alert that he had been before, his fingers gripping the arms of his leather seat.

"Why have you come to see me?"

Both the women looked at each other. This wasn't going as well as they had hoped for.

"This lady - Lisa - has moved into your old house, her husband has your old job."

With that comment Jeffrey leant forward and said -

"Tell your husband that he can keep my fucking job and you are both welcome to that fucking house, end of."

Sitting back again Jeffrey began picking and cleaning his nails, avoiding all eye contact and 'shutting up shop' until Lisa spoke again.

"Jeffrey, the man that Ronnie spoke of killed my daughter, we need to know, I need to know about your time at the house. Did you see anything strange when you lived there? Did any strange physical things happen to you?"

"That house is bad news" came the slow, deliberated reply. "And I ain't never going back there, ever."

Clearly agitated Jeffrey got up from his chair and started pacing up and down in the room, his feet reverberating on the solid wooden floor as his repeated path across the room and back quickened up. As he walked he clenched his right fist and punched it repeatedly into his left palm, in a rhythm with his footsteps. As he marched up and down his face started to redden and within a few strides across the room and back, he looked like his blood pressure was rising and he didn't look like the quiet and timid man who had only walked into the room five minutes before.

"You should not of come here" he screamed, still striding across the room, with his back towards them, then he turned around and said –

"Because he's come here with you…"

Lisa and Ronnie stared at each other in shock, with no idea of what to say. Then all of a sudden the whole atmosphere in the room changed.

The suns rays from the skylight above began to fade and the room was rapidly plunged into semi-darkness.

Jeffrey stopped walking and sat back down opposite them.

"This is just like when I lived at *that* house. I couldn't sleep. The children ran around all the time in my home, up and down the stairs, moving things and knocking my ornaments over – it was a living nightmare. Then there was that woman and that man. Every time I came down to my kitchen in the evening, they were sat at the table, always staring at me, always smiling, it was just so unnerving."

The two women stared at Jeffrey as he then leant forward in his chair.

"Then there was that man and what he did."

As soon as these words spilled out of Jeffrey's lips the sky outside turned dark and a lightning bolt flashed across the heavens, lighting his face and casting shadows across the room.

Jeffrey's face had altered and just for a second, both Lisa and Ronnie saw the snarling angry appearance of Isaiah Clevedon, mocking them, his spirit briefly controlling Jeffrey. Then he took full control of Jeffrey and he drooled as he started to speak.

"You've come to see this poor unfortunate and he is too weak to avoid me. He cannot control his own body, he's pathetic, he's tired and he's easy for manipulation. You think that he will help you? You think he'll give you answers? You think he's in control of his own body? Think again!!!"

The door was then flung open and Sam Wells was standing, framed by the opening and staring at what was taking place.

"This happens all the time," he shouted over the storm that was blowing outside and trying to drown out his voice in the room.

"We get this kind of 'demonic possession' here several times a year, it's usual the most susceptible of the patients, those that think they are seeing 'visions', it's never happened with Jeffrey before, he's too sensible to think he's being controlled."

Lisa and Ronnie were both sitting back in their seats, terrified. They had seen what had happened, Sam had not. Ronnie was back at school and remembering the caretaker taking 'care' of her and Lisa was seeing the man that she had seen reflected in her mirrors at her house.

Then his face almost flickered, like a television set with a poor reception and once again he was back to Jeffrey Walsh, looking confused, bewildered and someone recently influenced by some outside force.

"Time to go back to your room now Jeffrey," said Sam, helping him up out of the seat and shuffling him towards the door to the hallway. Lisa – now standing - tried to crack a smile, as a goodbye, to the poor defenceless soul and Ronnie gave the briefest of waves goodbye, from her seat.

Then as Sam was leading him through the doorway Jeffrey looked over his shoulder and said to Lisa –

"I loved your last daughter, I'm so glad that you have another as well. I'll be seeing you…" and with that he was gone through the door and Jeffrey and Sam walked the hallway back to his room, heading away from Meeting Room 5.

Thirty-One

The drive back to Eden lodge was silent.

Both women were equally distraught at what they had just encountered. Inside Lisa felt sick to the bone; she knew that this vile creature would be coming after Sandra. She was scared.

As they pulled up to the driveway, Lisa turned and said to Ronnie,

“What are we going to do?” to which Ronnie replied,

“I don't know Lisa, this has stirred up everything that I have tried to suppress for such a long time, I am just as scared as you are”.

Lisa sighed and opened the door to Ronnie’s SUV and got out. The feeling of uneasiness hung on to her like an anvil around her neck.

Lisa looked at the lodge; it had lost its appeal to her now, the rustic look of the wooden timbers seemed dark and morose, while the large windows with their arched tops seemed to be grinning at her. The house itself looked evil, and the memories that she hoped to create had turned all but sour.

“Do you want to come in for a drink” Lisa said, hoping that Ronnie would decline as she was asking out of common courtesy, she didn’t feel like having any more company.

“No, I won’t Lisa, I have stuff to do, besides its getting late and I want to get home before it gets dark, but thank you for the offer”.

Lisa smiled half-heartedly and closed the door. She stood and watched as Ronnie disappeared around the bend and out of sight, before making her way inside to her husband and Sandra.

****

Ronnie left the dirt track to Eden lodge and made her way down highway 15. It would only be another half hour or so before the day gave way to the night, and it looked like another storm was brewing. The cold red rays of the sun wavered as they diminished behind the thick bulbous grey clouds that enclosed on the day's dying light. Everything felt cold. Ronnie couldn't help but dwell upon her experience that afternoon; it made her feel vulnerable, a feeling that she had not experienced in a very long time. She shuddered at the thought of it, as her eyes began to well up.

"No Ronnie,'" she said out loud, "You must pull yourself together, you must stay strong", but it was hard.

Ronnie carried on down the road, the lights of a sixteen wheeler illuminated the car as it hurled on by her, pebble dashing the side of the car with loose stones. She glanced in her rear-view mirror as the lorry passed, its red rear lights like demonic eyes, got smaller and smaller as the distance between the two of them increased. As she turned her head forward again to look at the road ahead, a dark figure stood the centre of the road.

Ronnie slammed hard on the brakes but knew it was inevitable that she was going to collide.

"Holy Shit", she screamed, as smoke billowed out from both sets of tyres on her SUV.

The car skidded and swerved, and Ronnie struggled to maintain control of the wheel as she snaked either side of the road. The figure remained in the middle of the road, unable or unwilling to move out of the way of the oncoming vehicle. At the last moment before impact, Ronnie closed her eyes in anticipation of the impact.

The car came to a stop as Ronnie gripped the wheel in fear. The engine still ticked over as black billowing fumes of cancerous smoke belched out from the exhaust and disappeared into the darkness that was approaching. Ronnie released her grip from the wheel and opened her eyes expecting to see remnants of blood and bone on her windshield. To her surprise and relief, there was nothing. She looked in her mirror, the road behind was clear, and there was nothing out of the ordinary. Ronnie rested her head back on the seat, her heart pounded, and beads of sweat ran down her forehead and dripped down into the cleavage of her breasts. She suddenly shot forward,

"Oh Christ" she said out loud, just realising that whoever she hit may be trapped under the vehicle. Ronnie jumped out of the car and sprang down on all fours to look underneath, to her relief it was clear.

The door closed behind. Ronnie sat for a couple of moments to gather her thoughts and her wits; she must have been seeing things she thought, no doubt the stress of the day was getting to her. The locks clicked shut. Ronnie turned and looked, confused, as she hadn't moved an inch. Cold air rushed through the inside of her car; she gasped as a wave of iciness ran across her entire body giving her goosebumps and making her nipples go hard. It was then she heard the voice.

"Did you miss me? I've missed you little Ronnie."

Frozen with fear and unable to move, she could sense a presence in the back of the car. Ronnie began to cry as she felt the cold breath whisper in her ear.

"What do you want from me?" she screamed, only to be met with an unholy laugh.

She gasped as two invisible hands wrapped around her body and clung heavily to her breasts, its invisible squeeze getting tighter and tighter until Ronnie was struggling to draw breath. The seat shot backwards so that she was now in a lying position; a heaviness descended on to her as her eyes bulged with the pressure. Suddenly the grip around her chest released, still unable to move, Ronnie grabbed for every molecule of oxygen she could muster. She lay there paralysed, chest burning and heart pounding. Her eyes shot to and fro hoping to catch sight of what was in the car with her, but she already knew what was inside.

Ronnie screamed as both legs were pulled wide apart by invisible hands, the buttons on her blouse pinged off one by one, exposing her large breasts to the open air. Tears dampened the cups of her bra as she could feel her underwear slowly been pulled down her shaking legs until they dropped in the footwell beside her. Ronnie's back arched as something knife-like tore deep inside of her. It was then he made himself visible.

Hovering over her, Isaiah Clevedon's ghost, his teeth stained black and yellow, grinned at his former victim as he thrust his ghostly penis deep inside of her. Ronnie felt the sting with each thrust as her body bucked and contorted, her breasts flopped from side to side as the tension mounted, she closed her eyes and prayed for it to end.

Ronnie struggled to open her eyes, although the attack had now dissipated, she could still feel his presence around her. Every muscle in her body screamed with pain, as her hands and legs convulsed into an epileptic type fit. She glanced down through bloodshot eyes, her veins once a darkened red now flowed with the poison of her unholy attacker. The scars that had once before healed over, were now burning bright red, as thick black porous liquid seeped out from the initials 'I.C.'.

Ronnie felt the life draining out of her. Her breathing became shallower and shallower as the air inside her lungs turned to a noxious gas, her eyes became heavy and as darkness began to greet her, last words she heard before life escaped her was –

"***WELCOME TO MY WORLD BITCH!***"

Thirty-Two

The call came in a little after midnight, Sheriff Dawson and Officer Martinez were on night three out of four-night shifts, and both of them were back at the station.

"Come on Martinez, possible suicide on route 15, young lady in a car".

Both police officers were glad of the call, as they both had enough of doing paperwork. They made their way to the cruiser, and before long they were on their way to the scene.

The cruiser pulled up along the side of the road, they left the lights flashing to warn other potential drivers of their presence, but at this time of night other vehicles were few and far between. Sheriff Dawson flashed his torch on the SUV and recognised the number plate.

"That's Ronnie Rydall's car," he said to his partner. Both of them drew their weapons and slowly made their way towards the front, calling out her name. Sheriff Dawson shined his torch in the driver's side window. He immediately jumped backwards at what he saw.

Ronnie Rydall's lifeless body lay flat in the front seat. Her body, white in complexion had black lines running from the tips of her feet right up to the top of her head.

Officer Martinez gasped, "what the fuck is that on her?"

"I don't know" came the reply from the Sheriff.

Martinez reached inside her belt and pulled out a pair of light blue rubber gloves before opening the door.

"Shit boss, it's locked from the inside".

The Sheriff shone his torch on the ignition, her keys were still in there, and all the windows were locked. Something didn't add up as it was clear that Ronnie had been sexually assaulted, but they were unsure of how.

The sheriff went back to his cruiser to get his magic set of keys out. A set of skeleton keys issued to him, which always came in handy. After a couple of failed attempts at opening the door to the car, the lock finally clicked open. As they opened the door, a rotting smell so vile blasted them in the face, causing Martinez to run to the side and vomit.

"Jesus boss, what the hell is that smell?"

"I don't know" came his reply.

He took out a well-used handkerchief and pressed it firmly over his nose and mouth. Protocol said he had to check for signs of life, even if he knew that she was dead. He placed two fingers on the side of Ronnie's neck. Her skin was ice cold to the touch; she was dead all right. The black lines that they had seen from outside the car window were now clearly visible, it was her veins, but Sheriff Dawson had never seen anything like this before. All of Ronnie's veins were bulging black and looked like a road map across her whole body. Then he noticed the letters. In the thick black, red angry looking scars, the initials I.C peered out from the dried bloodstains. Both the Sheriff and Martinez looked at each other in shock.

"Boss, that can't be Isaiah, it's impossible", but among all the strange events and occurrences that were happening as of late, they were not quite sure what was real anymore.

The Sheriff told Martinez to call it in.

****

Following morning Lisa was in the kitchen preparing Sandra's and Jonathan's breakfast. She could sense something was wrong, but she couldn't quite put her finger on it. She turned to Jonathan, who sat at the table looking like something the cat dragged in, unshaven and unkempt, but that was by far the least of Lisa's concerns at that moment in time.

"How are you feeling today honey?"

Jonathan yawned and ruffled his hair to wake himself up a bit more,

"I feel better today than yesterday, it's those damn pills that are killing me".

A car turning the bend and heading towards the lodge broke Lisa's attention from her husband. It was the Sheriff. Lisa went to the door and opened it as both police officers got out.

"Hello Mrs Matthews, how are you today?," said Martinez.

"I am doing ok thank you. To what do I owe the pleasure of this visit?"

"We are here on official police business I'm afraid" said the Sheriff.

Lisa looked perplexed and invited both of them inside. Jonathan got up from the table to greet their two guests but was regretting it almost immediately, as pain shot up his leg.

"Please Mr Matthews, remain seated".

Jonathan sat back down with a thud and gladly adhered to the Sheriff's request. The sheriff turned to Lisa who stood by the kitchen sink nursing a lukewarm cup of coffee.

"Mrs Matthews, I understand you visited Ms Rydall yesterday, at what time did you meet her?"

Lisa put the coffee cup on the side and turned to the Sheriff,

"Ronnie! Why? What's the matter?"

Sheriff Dawson informed Lisa that unfortunately Ms Rydall was attacked sometime during the evening and that she had passed away.

Lisa felt her legs go like jelly and had to hold on to the sink for support.

"Ronnies dead" she exclaimed. "What? How?"

"Please Mrs Matthews, what time did you leave her?".

Lisa began telling both officers about their trip to see Jeffrey Walsh and what had occurred during their meeting. After Lisa had finished telling them what had happened, Sandra walked into the kitchen.

"It was the bad man mommy, he killed your friend".

Lisa was in shock. She remembered what Jeffrey Walsh had said about the entity following them. Lisa looked at the Sheriff with a concerned look upon her face.

"It's okay, I know all about Isaiah Clevedon, and what became of him."

The Sheriff turned to Martinez who was kneeling beside Lisa's daughter looking at a drawing she had just finished.

"What have you here, little lady?" Martinez said.

Sandra smiled and said "It's a picture of my family."

Martinez took the picture from Sandra and glared at what she saw on the paper in front of her. Mommy, Daddy, me, Kimmie, Hyacinth and Emily. There was nothing very odd about the names itself; it was what Sandra had drawn above them that concerned her. Above the crude drawing of the Matthews family and the other two girls, who Martinez put down to a child's active imagination, was a figure done in all black. Its eyes were coloured red, and he was wearing what could only be described as blue overalls, bearing the initials I.C. 'the Bad Man', in black lettering across the front of the paper.

Lisa's face turned to a look of anguish.

"That Bastard killed my daughter".

Jonathan was shocked that his wife would use such profanities in front of their daughter, but Lisa just gave him an angry look, knowing that he disapproved. Sheriff Dawson shook his head.

"Despite what you may or may not know about Isaiah Clevedon and what happened to him, it was over twenty years ago, and he is long dead."

But before he had a chance to finish up what he was saying, Officer Martinez said,

"Oh come on boss, that fucker is back, there is no denying it." The Sheriff was none too pleased with his colleague's outburst but was resigned to the fact that she was right.

Thirty-Three

The rain had been pouring outside for an hour. Not just a short burst, but a continual torrential downpour, that seemed to have no intentions of easing up.

It was now just a little after 2am and Lisa was lying in bed listening to the rain. The sound of the constant rush of water was trying to compete with Jonathan's snoring and neither was winning. But the only person that was actually losing was Lisa and she was fighting against the noises to try and get some sleep. All she could think about was Ronnie and how Clevedon had taken another person close to her away, something would need to be done. If this carried on she could see herself ending up in Waverley House with Jeffrey Walsh.

Looking at the ceiling, she eventually closed her eyes and tried to count sheep – white fluffy bundles of joy – but to no avail, they gradually all escaped and ran off into the next field and she couldn't imagine where they were or what they were possible doing, '*sheep stuff*' she thought to herself.

Twenty minutes later she sat up in bed and said out loud, just in case Jonathan was listening in between snores.

"I'm going downstairs to get a drink of water, do you want anything?"

The lack of reply from her husband made her take this as a 'no', so she quietly crept out of bed and left their room and began to walk along the hallway.

She checked in on Sandra to make sure all was ok, as she now did most nights, since the ‘event’ had taken place. She felt at times that she was being over protective, but in her mind she knew that she was doing the right thing, she really didn’t want to lose another daughter.

Sandra was tucked up in bed, but with one leg hanging out of the covers, trying to escape the temperature under the quilt and surprisingly Rex was sat at the foot of her bed staring at Sandra.

None of them had seen Rex for over two months. Lisa had assumed that he had been poorly and had either crawled off to die somewhere or someone had buried him, having ploughed into him on one of the local roads on the island.

Lisa walked over to give Rex a smooth and he was as friendly and receptive to some petting as much as he ever was. He seemed to be clean and healthy and well fed, so he must have been being fed by one of the neighbours or living off his wiles in the wild – though the former seemed to be the more obvious option, especially as he was quite a lazy cat.

Rex began to purr loudly, sounding like a little outboard motor on a very tiny boat, as Lisa continued to rub and smooth him up and down his back and sides.

Sandra began to stir as she became aware of Rex’s purring.

“Mommy Rex is back. He hasn’t run away, he’s back, he’s back.”

“Yes darling, he’s back and he’s here to stay, now you turn over and I will go down and find Rex some tuna fish to have, as we don’t have any cat food left”

With that Sandra rolled over and Lisa threw the bed covers back over her, making sure that she was warm and away from the effects of the elements that were still going crazy outside the window.

As she left the room she looked back at Sandra.

If she had to, she would do this every evening until Sandra left and got married, but that was a small price to pay to keep her daughter; if only she had heard Kimmie being attacked, their little family would then still be a whole group, instead of a fractured version.

Just as Lisa pulled the door a little more shut, Rex squeezed out through the gap, between the brightly painted door and the exposed wood doorframe and followed Lisa along the hallway and down the stairs towards the kitchen.

Just as they were nearing the kitchen and off the bottom steps of the stairs, Rex slowly backed up. His back arched and he hissed and spat really loudly, making Lisa jump. Since the 'event' Lisa had been living on the edge, her nerves shot. She had been to the doctor to get something, but all he gave her were 'anti-depressants' and they didn't appear to be even scraping the surface or doing anything.

"What's the matter boy?" she asked bending down to stroke him, but Rex would not walk any closer to the kitchen and stood rooted to the spot.

"Do you want some fishy?"

At that moment Rex turned and ran up the stairs once more. Bounding up as fast as he could, taking two steps at a time – something seemed to have bothered him and Lisa was hoping that it wasn't a return of Isaiah Clevedon, she'd seen enough of him for a lifetime already.

As she walked closer towards the kitchen, the temperature began to drop with each step. Each further footstep another few degrees dropped, until she could see her breath, like cloudy steam, in the light shining in from the full moon outside.

Then she entered the kitchen and saw what was freaking Rex out and dropping the temperature.

There were two people sat at her kitchen table, sitting side by side, shimmering in the light.

Thirty-Four

The two people at the table looked around at Lisa as she stared at them. They flickered and glistened in the light as they both smiled at each other, sat at her table, without a care in the world. The ghostly pair then both in unison turned their heads to look full on at Lisa.

Lisa's stomach churned and she began to feel very sick as she looked at the two burnt and charred bodies sat in her kitchen, looking like they felt that they should be there, that they belonged there. Although the room was now deathly cold, the temperature having dropped to just above freezing, sweat from fear still dripped from her forehead, passing rapidly across her cheeks, down over her chin, finally ending in a damp ever expanding patch on the top of her bedtime top.

The man was probably in his late 40's, the woman was of a similar age and they both looked grotesquely disfigured, as they each tried to break into a smile in Lisa's direction. Both sets of teeth were clearly visible, where their cheeks and lips had been burnt away in what must have been a powerful fire. Each persons eye sockets were empty, gaping black holes of nothingness, their eyeballs boiled away from the heat of the flames, as they had licked and tore at their faces. Their cheekbones shone in the moonlight, as their skeletal hands reached to each other, the bony fingers interlacing in what would normally have been a very romantic interlude, if they didn't look so terrifying. Their hair was singed and remained only in charred tufts, the man's not as badly damaged as the woman's.

The clothing that they both were wearing were charred rags; the man in what would have been a white formal work-shirt, dark waistcoat and black trousers, her in a long flowing ankle length dress with the remnants of an apron hanging over the front, all now both tattered and covered with black smudges from smoke and flame damage. Although the clothes were damaged beyond repair, Lisa guessed that they were 'of an age', meaning that these apparitions were not of the recently deceased, but from at least one hundred years before, the clothes looking like something from the end of the 1800's

Their heads then turned back leisurely to each other, their jaws moving in harmony as they leant in for a romantic kiss, which looked all the more ghoulish for the near total lack of skin and all of the glistening and shiny bone on display.

Lisa noticed a noise and then she realised that it was her breathing and the loud beating of her heart, thudding rapidly in her chest and the sound of the blood rhythmically pumping in her ears.

Then they both slowly turned back to her, their vacant eye sockets, giving an empty gaze, stared in her direction, but with a lack of focus, making it difficult for Lisa to judge if the two spirits were 'good or evil'. Just as she continued to look at them, their voices loud and booming, reverberated around the walls, in an echoing tone, both said –

"We need to talk with you, Lisa…"

Thirty-Five

Lisa was terrified.

As she stood at the edge of the kitchen, - *her kitchen, in her house* – half on the rug, half on the smoothly polished floorboards, she felt compelled to walk a few steps closer to the two apparitions, that were sat at her kitchen table and take a seat opposite them. As she seated herself down, the ghosts seemed to smile at her, which was more than a little unnerving, as the smile looked more like a sneer, due to the lack of skin and mass on the bones, their teeth glinting and sparkling in the moonlight.

"We've been wanting to help you Lisa…" said the female gesturing her hands towards her in a pleading, helpful motion.

"We cannot let you be alone in this…" continued the male, resting his skeletal hand on the females hand and rubbing hers with his long bony fingers, in a sure sign that love was still a definite possibility in the hereafter.

Behind them in the lounge the old grandfather clock chimed at 3am, the Devil's hour, the 'witching hour'. Lisa knew that this time was rumoured to be time most associated with supernatural events and 'happenings' and at the moment, she didn't doubt this at all, seeing what was before her own eyes as positive proof. As the third and final chime echoed around the ground floor of Eden Lodge, she heard her husband stirring upstairs, rolling over in bed and knocking a pillow onto the floor with a soft thud – she couldn't believe that he was missing what was happening on their ground floor.

The noise from her bedroom disturbed Rex, still on the top of the stairs, terrified to move and going nowhere near the kitchen; to tell the truth Rex was ready to leave the house once more and go off on one of his month long wanders around the nearby neighbourhood and possibly return when the apparitions had once again vacated his home.

"Our daughters have tried to help you all…" the man said as he continued to massage his 'partners' hand, ***"but you didn't believe in them or want their help…"***

"Hyacinth and Emily have been here all the time with you and they have played with your children from day one – they are playing with Kimmie now…" replied the woman moving in her chair, leaning in towards the man and putting her left arm around his emaciated and gaunt frame.

Lisa smiled at the thought of her recently deceased daughter being happy and looked after. She had always hoped that there was life after death and somewhere to go where some peace would eventually be granted after the stresses of modern day life and the heartaches of illnesses and sudden deaths. Then, as if on queue, the two young girls glided silently into the room on a light breeze, their feet not even touching the floorboards or the rugs on the floor and following close behind them was Kimmie. Dressed in her nightwear – the last clothes she had worn - Kimmie shone with a ghostly sheen – just like the others - as she floated in noiselessly, close on the heels of the two young girls and came to rest near the kitchen table, smiling at her mother.

"Don't worry Mommy, I'm OK.

Hyacinth and Emily are looking after me and their Mommy and Daddy are taking care of us all and keeping the 'bad man' away…'

The tears quickly welled up in Lisa's eyes as she looked at the 'see through' ghostly version of her eldest daughter. Although she had passed away, it was a relief for Lisa to see her and it appeared that she was being cared for in the afterlife. She almost felt like going and waking both Jonathan and Sandra, but it might cause them even more heartache and only one of the family in this eerie situation, was probably for the best.

"The man is coming to cause you much more anguish and despair – Isaiah Clevedon is coming soon as you are in his home, the

place that he has claimed as his own, since he was taken over into the spirit world..." said the children's father as he tried to explain to Lisa, what was happening and the reasons why, since they had all moved in to Eden Lodge.

Lisa stood listening to the voice as it echoed around her home, the jaws moving as the words drifted out towards her, over skinless lips.

The father talked on for a time, explaining all about the evil spirit of Isaiah Clevedon and why he did what he did and why he was now doing, what he was now doing.

As the peaceful voice carried on, Lisa found herself beginning to drift off to sleep, her eyes getting heavy and her body feeling exhausted. It was like listening down a tunnel, the voice was still there, but became more and more distant as it went on and on and on...

"Are you alright?" asked Jonathan as he brushed the hair off Lisa's face and gently caressed her cheek with his hand.

Lisa looked at her husband. She was back in her bed, but had she been dreaming or had she really had the encounter downstairs?

No, it had happened and she knew it and now she knew exactly what she had to do.

They had to exorcise the spirit of Isaiah Clevedon and cleanse the house and the local area of his evil...

Thirty-Six

The following morning, Jonathan woke up before Lisa.

The pain in his leg was more aching than burning now, and he too saw this as a good sign that his body was starting the healing process. He turned to Lisa, who was in a deep sleep and kissed her on the forehead,

"I love you" he said in a whispered voice so as he wouldn't wake her.

Jonathan climbed out of bed and shivered as his bare feet touched the cold floorboards beneath them. He hopped over to where his dressing gown was, his limp was much more obvious when the cold got to his bones, and he suspected he would no doubt at some point get arthritis, but he would carry on until he couldn't do anymore.

After fumbling with his dressing gown and going to the toilet, Jonathan made his way into Sandra's room. The door creaked open, and he stuck his head around the corner, she was still sleeping soundly, and the light from outside crept in between the pulled curtains, showering Sandra's sleeping body in a halo of gold. He smiled to himself, which was something that he hadn't done since before Kimmie passed away. He realised how hard it all must be on Lisa and Sandra, and he could feel himself well up with tears, but managed to fight them back. He closed the door to Sandra's room and tiptoed towards the stairs. Jonathan had no idea what time of the morning it was, but he knew he needed coffee regardless.

****

Jonathan walked into the kitchen and headed over to make a pot of coffee. The air felt stale and muggy like all the fresh air had been sucked out and replaced with fumes of a thousand sweaty armpits. Rex was curled on one of the chairs, awake but not bothering to move from his warm resting place.

"Good morning you daft cat," he said as he walked towards the windows to let some well needed clean air in, but all the cat did was yawn and close his eyes once more. Jonathan opened both of the windows and instantly cool crisp morning air swirled around him, although it was cold, it was refreshing at the same time. Jonathan stood for a moment and inhaled two great lungful's of oxygen and gasped with relief as his body reacted to the freshness. But then something changed, something unexplainable, something horrible.

As Jonathan turned to sit down at the table to drink his coffee, he suddenly froze, he was stunned, paralysed, and unable to take another step forward or move his arms. It scared him. The fresh air that he had just let in was now thick and muggy like a thick soup, which stuck in his throat. He could feel he wasn't alone, whatever or whoever it was that was with him surrounded him from every direction, yet still all he could see was a dark shadow, a flicker as it dashed on by his eyes.

Then it went dark.

****

Sandra opened her eyes to see Rex laying beside her. His gentle meows and nudges of affection brought a smile to her face; he was her only friend now that her sister had passed, her only living friend that is. Sandra ran her hand down the length of the cat's back and giggled as he arched it lovingly. She needed to pee, but was reluctant to spoil the moment in time, eventually she clambered out of her bed disturbing the feline in the process. As Sandra opened the door to walk to the bathroom she could see her dad standing outside his and her mum's bedroom. He was still, motionless and didn't turn to acknowledge Sandra. Once again the cat appeared and started hissing and growling, its fur stood on end as it felt the malevolence in the air. The cat darted past Sandra and straight down the stairs.

Sandra stood confused as to what was wrong with her dad. She hesitantly called his name to see if he was ok. Jonathan turned his head towards his daughter, Sandra gasped and started to walk back into her bedroom.

Whatever it was, that was not her father.

As Sandra closed the door behind her and quickly dived back into the bed, she pulled the covers up over her head and started praying. She didn't like this one bit and was expecting her dad to burst into the bedroom at any minute, but he never did.

Jonathan pushed the door to where his wife was sleeping. It bounced off the wall with a thud as he stepped forward. The noise of the door banging stirred Lisa from her sleep.

Jonathan was standing at the foot of the bed in silence.

Lisa quickly sat up and realised something wasn't right.

"Jonathan, what's the matter?" Lisa gasped, all her deep-seated intuitions were now screaming at her to get the hell out of Dodge. Jonathan's eyes stared blankly at his wife before raising his hand above his head.

"OH SHIT" Lisa said as she noticed the claw hammer in her husband's hand.

"This can't be happening, Jonathan, please, what are you doing?"

Her husband opened his mouth to speak, but what came out of it was surely not her husband. The voice, a deep angry growl, snarled at Lisa.

"You fucking bitch, fucking bitch".

It was then that Lisa knew exactly what was happening to her husband. That bastard Clevedon had taken control of Jonathan and was about to smash her head in with a hammer. Lisa had to think fast.

Lisa jumped up out of bed. Her body didn't register the coldness on her naked body as adrenaline coursed through her system. The lamp on the bedside table was heavy, and she was reluctant to strike her husband, but given the circumstances she felt like she had no choice.

The base of the lamp came down hard on Jonathan's nose. Blood and snot exploded across his face as the bone instantly broke. Jonathan yelped and dropped the hammer by Lisa's feet. Without even thinking,

Lisa ran as fast as she could at her husband and speared him. Jonathan let out a gasp of air as his body buckled under the pressure of his diving wife and instantly fell hard onto the bedroom floor. Blood seeped onto the back of Lisa's head and shoulders as she scrambled to get off her husbands writhing body. Lisa managed to scramble and roll away towards the bed landing a swift kick to Jonathan's groin in the process. Lisa stood up and ran to the other side of the room and watched as Jonathan had both hands cupped over his broken nose and was heaving for breath. Blood oozed from between his fingers and ran down the length of his arm. Tears blinded him, and he reached a hand out just as Lisa swiftly dashed on by him.

Lisa ran for the door, she had one concern now, and that was her daughter. She heard a thud coming from behind but was reluctant to turn and look, until she heard her husband calling for her. She stopped, her chest heaving and her nipples erect, her body now registering the coldness that was in the air. Jonathan was sat on the bedroom floor leaning against the bed still holding his busted nose. The look of sheer horror on her husbands face would stay with Lisa the rest of her life. Clevedon had left his body.

Jonathan was himself once more.

Thirty-Seven

Sandra slowly opened the bedroom door and peeked out. She could hear talking coming from her parents' room and quickly ran to them. Jonathan was now sitting on the bed with his head tilted back pressing a cloth to his face. Lisa turned to her daughter and said:

"It's ok honey, daddy just fell out of bed".

Sandra began to cry at the sight of her father covered in copious amounts of blood.

"Why did daddy want to hurt you, mummy?"

Lisa held her arms out for Sandra to come and give her a hug, which she gladly obliged. As Sandra nestled into her mother's chest she began to whimper; fresh tears welled in Lisa's eyes as Sandra turned to look at her mother,

"Was it the bad man again mummy?"

Lisa ran her hand through the top of her daughter's hair and kissed her on the forehead. Reluctantly she hated lying to her daughter but felt this was for the best, she was already scared enough and had been through enough trauma these past couple of months to be dealing with such an immense situation.

"Not at all honey, daddy just had a bad nightmare and fell out of bed, that's all".

The bleeding to Jonathan's nose was starting to stop, but the swelling was causing him a lot of discomfort and making it difficult for him to breathe. His eyes were beginning to swell shut, and he looked like something that Rex the cat would have brought in.

"It's ok Sandra", Jonathan said as he removed the bloodied cloth from his face. Sandra thought he looked funny as his nose jilted out to the left of his face. Jonathan managed to crack a smile, if only for his daughter's sake.

Lisa told Sandra to go ahead and get dressed that the three of them were going to go into town today, this came as a surprise to Jonathan as he was in no mood or fit state to go anywhere. Sandra acknowledged her mother's wishes and went into her room to get dressed. A Sandra left the room, Lisa turned to Jonathan, and before he had a chance to say anything, Lisa began to ascertain the plans that she had meticulously conjured.

"I know it's not what you want to do Jonathan, but we have to do something, you could have killed…"

Before Lisa finished her sentence Jonathan stood up, he had his hands raised to his chest and a pissed off look upon his face.

"Oh wait a minute Lisa, I could have killed you? That wasn't me, and you know full well that I would never lay a hand on you or Sandra".

Lisa averted her eyes towards the bedroom floor,

"Jonathan, I know you would never intentionally inflict any harm to Sandra or me, but this fucking ghost is only getting stronger, next time we may not be so lucky".

Jonathan sat back down on the bed and realised that what his wife was saying was right; he could never live with himself if he ever hurt his family, ghost or not.

"Ok, but I doubt I will be able to do much walking, and besides I look like the elephant man."

Lisa smiled at her husband and said sorry for hitting him so hard, Jonathan leaned forward and kissed her, the taste of blood still strong on his lips, but Lisa didn't care.

****

Lisa, Jonathan and Sandra got into the old station wagon. Jonathan was still in no fit state to drive, so the responsibility fell with Lisa.

"It looks like that storm is finally passing us by,"' Jonathan said, he was contemplating going to the hospital to get his nose manipulated back into place but knew that his family needed him, even if he was a cripple.

Lisa drove down route 15 and turned the bend towards the old bridge that led into town. Sandra was peering out of the window, trying to count the trees as the car sped on by them. As they reached the small incline leading up to the bridge, Sandra noticed a figure peering from the bushes. His blue overalls were not in contrast to the amber, browns and greens of the woods, so he stuck out like a sore thumb. Sandra gasped as the car drove past him. The figure smiled at her, as she so desperately wanted to turn and look away, but some unforeseen force compelled her to stare at him. Blood seemed to be running down from his forehead painting his grey-white skin a dark red. Sandra knew who it was. And just like that, the figure disappeared.

The Matthews family pulled up into the parking lot; the town was relatively busy given it was a Thursday. Lisa parked up and turned to her husband,

"Jonathan, you take Sandra into the cafe and get a bite to eat, I am going to go to the church and try and speak to the priest, he may be able to help us or at least point us in the right direction".

Jonathan acknowledged his wife's requests, and tucked a baseball cap on his head to try and cover up the bulbous snout he was now sporting, and both he and Sandra scuttled out of the car and limped towards the cafe on the other side of the road, holding his daughter's hand.

Thirty-Eight

Back at Eden Lodge, everything lay still and quiet. Rex was laying by the window peering out into the back towards the woods, occasionally turning his attention to licking his paws and cleaning the top of his head. Outside clouds began to congregate above the lodge, casting a blanket of darkness as they blocked out the sun. The cat suddenly became aware of a presence within the house. His eyes glared, as his body, frozen and stiff, watched as something began to stir from across the room. A dark mass spilt out onto the walls of the kitchen, its malevolence, infecting the very air it possessed. Rex scarpered for the small opened window beside the door and quickly shot out through the gap.

****

Lisa made her way down the main street of the town towards the only other church that the town possessed. She knew the church where Kimmie's funeral was held had been closed these past few weeks for repairs. Although she was never a religious person, she was soon starting to become one. St David's of the Evangelical church was nestled in behind a small cluster of shops. The church itself was only a couple of hundred years old and its architecture reflected as such. Sunlight dazzled off the stained glass windows giving the coloured panes a rainbow effect. The main doors to the church were thick varnished-mahogany and almost reached the top to the roof. Two heavy bronze rings donned the outside of the well-weathered wood, giving it the old rustic look you'd expect from old churches. The doors were open, and Lisa stepped inside.

Lisa made her way up the aisle towards the front of the church; organ music echoed off it's harshly painted white walls and hung in the air. The smell of burning candles wafted up her nose, almost making her sneeze. Two old ladies, one wearing a red headscarf and black blouse and the other dressed in a white floral dress, were kneeling by a pew deep in prayer, seemingly unaware to Lisa's presence. Across the front of the altar, rows of fresh-cut flowers were neatly laid out in rows in front of the pulpit, and a small microphone and stand stood where the priest gave his sermon.

Lisa stopped for a moment to get her bearings, she was looking for the door to the vestry, and although she felt out of place she knew this was something she needed to do. Her family depended on it.

Lisa took the three steps up that led to the back of the altar and headed for the back. The door to the vestry was set back in an alcove to the left. She glanced back at the two women who were praying, and the one with the red headscarf was now sat up rummaging through her handbag, eventually retrieving two hard toffees, one for herself and the other for her friend. Lisa walked to the door and stood for a moment, how was she going to play this out? She thought about it for a few moments, then knocked on the door twice.

Father Murry was sat at the desk sipping on a freshly made tea going over his mass for that evening.

As he read out loud the remembrances for Myrtle Heath and Cathryn Gilmore, he heard a knock on the door. He put his cup down and said,

"Please come in."

Lisa took a deep breath and turned the handle and entered the room. Lisa was surprised at how small and cluttered the vestry was. Piles of books and leaflets were stacked up on either side of the wooden desk. A small stereo sat on a sideboard with discarded CD's, most of them without cases, dotted around the stereo. A dusty framed picture of Elvis Presley sat at the back of the sideboard. Father Murry noticed his guest staring at the picture,

"Ahh he is the only other God in my life, that and the big man up above".

He stood up and offered Lisa his hand, which she kindly took.

"Please take a seat; I am Father Murry, I don't believe I've had the pleasure of meeting you before".

Lisa smiled and took the only other seat available and sat opposite the priest. She was nervous, and the shaking of her legs indicated as much.

"How may I help you, mam?"

Lisa introduced herself to the priest and where and with whom she lived, before telling him the occurrences of what was happening at Eden Lodge.

Father Murry was well aware of the name Isaiah Clevedon.

With the town being so close-knit as it was, a tragedy such as the abuse Clevedon had caused would stick around for a lifetime. The priest sat back in his chair and was silent for a few moments before speaking.

"And you're telling me that the ghost of Isaiah Clevedon has already killed your daughter and has attacked your family?"

Lisa shifted awkwardly in her chair and nodded in acknowledgement.

Father Murry shifted his chair back and stood up. He walked towards a small window and stared out briefly before turning to Lisa.

"Are you asking me to perform an exorcism?" by now Lisa had a distraught but hopeful look about her.

"Yes, father, that is exactly what I am asking for you to do, I, we need your help".

Father Murry sat back down at the desk and opened up the good book on Mark 16:17, and read from the passage:

"And these signs shall follow them that believe; In my name shall they cast out devils; they shall speak with new tongues".

After he had finished reciting the words, he looked at Lisa.

"If I were to do this Mrs Matthews, I would need to get permission from the Vatican first".

Lisa looked disheartened,

"How long is that going to take father?"

Father Murry bowed his head.

"At least a couple of weeks."

Lisa despaired at the priest.

"Two weeks! We could be dead by then father. Is there nothing you can do to help us?"

Father Murry shook his head and apologised,

"I am sorry Mrs Matthews, but without the Vatican's authority my hands are tied".

The priest opened up a drawer that was in front of him and took out two items and handed them to Lisa.

"Take these Mrs Matthews; these will help you".

Father Murry handed Lisa the two items, a small crucifix and a vile of holy water.

"Splash this around your home; it may keep the evil at bay and buy you some time."

Tears began streaming down Lisa's face as she stood up to thank the priest.

"I will do what I can Mrs Matthews".

Lisa wiped the wetness from her eyes on her sleeve, turned and walked away from the priest.

Lisa took a slow walk back towards the main strip of the town to meet back up with her husband and her daughter. It had started raining again, and as she clutched the small cross and bottle in her hand, she found herself praying to God. Her hair clung to her face as cold rain pelted her from every direction. Lisa's soul was shattered as she thought to herself, how much more did she and her family have to take, and would the churches answer come before it was too late.

Only time would tell.

Thirty-Nine

Storm clouds were already steadily building over Martha's Vineyard as they made the short drive back to Eden Lodge. The dark skies filled with swirling clouds full of rain - and worse - appeared to be on the way.

Sandra was sat in the back playing some noisy game on her iPad, where small cats – wearing top hats and waistcoats - were attacking trees and plants and the sound of it was already beginning to grind Lisa's nerves. She was driving and Jonathan was fast asleep in the passenger seat, still highly dosed up on painkillers, a small frothy river of drool heading down his chin from the right side of his mouth.

Lisa leant forward and turned on the radio, but flicked it off again just a few seconds later due to only seeming to be able pick up interference and white noise – basically random beeps, crackles and occasional 'sound bites'.

Looking in the rear-view mirror she could see Sandra still smiling to herself and playing her game, unmindful of anything else in the world. Seeing that she was fairly content and reasonably quiet, Lisa's concentration began to wander as she carried on looking out at the road straight ahead.

'What if there was no way to get rid of Clevedon? What if they were stuck with him as long as they lived at their home? Would they leave the island and move back to Boston?'

"I'm not going anywhere..." came a now eerily familiar voice from behind her headrest, in the back of the car.

Looking at a reflection in the mirror she could see Isaiah Clevedon staring back at her, sat on the back seat, running his fingers gently through Sandra's hair - she seeming to be completely unaware of his presence right next to her.

Sccccccrrrrreeeeeeccccchhhhh!!!!

Lisa slammed on the brakes, everyone jolting forward as the SUV came to an immediate stop, stirring up a small dust bowl in the road, in the process.

"What have we hit?" slurred Jonathan sitting forward, as he tried his hardest to focus on the road ahead, his eyes still bleary and pink from the pills and the near continual sleeping.

"Mommy, have we killed an animal? Please don't tell me we've hurt something."

Lisa's eyes darted back to the mirror and now there was just her daughter sat in the back on her own, looking concerned. There was no pervert left in the car, but he had proved enough to Lisa, for her to know that he was still about and 'travelling' with them back once again to their home at Eden Lodge.

"No darling, we haven't hit anything," she said to Sandra, trying her hardest to smile and put her daughter at ease – but Lisa's anxiety levels were already peaking and she was already not in a good place.

"Sorry Jonathan, I guess I need to get some sleep as well," she continued, rubbing her eyes and patting her husband on his good leg. Jonathan smiled and his drooping eyelids closed once more as he drifted immediately back to sleep, his head lolling onto his chest, as his chin headed southwards.

Lisa fired the engine back up and the SUV moved forward heading home again. Within fifteen minutes Lisa pulled up outside their home and turned the engine off once more.

Sandra undid her seatbelt and climbed out as Lisa tried to wake Jonathan, him stirring like he was coming out of a deep sleep; the pills were certainly taking too much of a toll on him and the sooner he was off the medication the better in Lisa's eyes. She could understand that the pills were probably the only things that were keeping Jonathan positive, but they were detrimental to him being anything else – a fully functioning husband and father, as well as a working Ranger.

'I wonder how long they'll continue to pay him? Jeffrey Walsh was laid off after all...' thought Lisa to herself as she unbuckled her husbands seatbelt and helped him out of the car and they all moved off towards their home.

Sandra ran on up the steps and noticed that the door was open.

"Mommy we left the door unlocked."

Fear filled Lisa's mind as soon as she heard Sandra shout the message from the open doorway – a message or a warning?

Jonathan shook himself out of his stupor as he and Lisa walked up the steps, the old wood creaking as they both went up to the front door. The wood around the edges of the door was splintered and cracked, where someone had prized the door open, no key would be needed for them to get back in the house this time.

"Sandra, be a good girl and go back and stand by the car," Lisa told her daughter, fearing the worst as she and Jonathan threw the door open, the unoiled hinges creaking as the door swung fully open. Expecting to encounter a burglar or worse, they looked in through the open door, fearing that this would be another nightmare situation, of which they were encountering more and more since moving here.

As Sandra did as she was told and walked back to the car, Lisa and Jonathan walked into the house, the first thing that they saw was the graffiti. Amongst the random doodles and scribbles on the wall was a huge message, painted in large red letters –

'Die, Die, Isaiah Clevedon, Die Forever'

The darkness on the stairs – and enveloping the rest of the house - made no difference to the visibility of the lettering, as it stood out like a beacon in the gloom, it's message loud and clear, but if they'd been out who had done it? It couldn't have been kids and it couldn't have been locals because from Lisa's experience so far, children came nowhere near there house and the adults on the island all liked to keep it quiet about the deceased paedophile, the mere mention of his name dragging up the tragic events of the past.

As they walked further into the house, the graffiti became more prominent, reaching up the stairs and into the lounge and across all of the units in the kitchen – the house was an incredible mess, the paint would take days to clean up and to remove the feeling of their home being violated by intruders. Moving through the kitchen everything still seemed to be there, nothing was moved, nothing taken.

"Oh my god, my jewellery," said Lisa out loud as she thought of the necklaces and rings that were on her dressing table upstairs in their bedroom and began to move quickly towards the foot of the staircase.

"Slow down, let's get a little something to protect us first," replied Jonathan as he grabbed her arm and picked up a solid wooden rolling pin shaped like a miniature baseball bat and passed Lisa the iron, which was hanging on the end of the ironing board, just behind the kitchen door.

If they were still in the house, they would have a severe headache after the Matthews' had got hold of them.

Walking slowly up the stairs armed with their kitchen utensils, Lisa and Jonathan prepared themselves for a head to head meeting with their intruder or intruders, whoever they were.

The stairs groaned as they tried their best to walk up them quietly, the creaking drawing attention to themselves, moving towards the bedroom -their destination - and possible a showdown. Reaching the top of the stairs they slowly walked along the landing, passing Sandra's room and heading to their bedroom, the door slightly ajar.

"Here we go," whispered Jonathan as he prepared himself to enter the room, with Lisa standing right behind him looking like she was preparing to iron someone's shirts and not '*cave their head in*' with their Sunbeam Steam Master 1400.

Moving forward Jonathan flung the door open and they both ran into their bedroom, to be greeted with… 'nothing'.

Their bedroom looked exactly the same as when they had left it that morning. The bed was made, their clothes were still precariously balanced on the overflowing wicker wash-basket in the corner by the window and all of her jewellery was still on the ceramic hand statue on the dressing table – nothing was missing, no graffiti, no prowler.

All was just as it had been earlier that morning. No one had been in their bedroom since they'd been gone.

Then suddenly the room was lit up bright, like they were in a nightclub. Bright white, blue and red lights flashed around their bedroom, so dazzling in the semi-darkness that it almost gave them both an immediate migraine.

Both of them then ran down the stairs and went out the front door to see what was happening, but more importantly to check on Sandra.

As they looked at the car they could see that Sandra wasn't there. The first thought that went through Lisa's head was that she'd been taken, but then they turned to what had been the source of the flashing brightness.

Forty

Coming quickly up their drive was the local Sherriff's car.

Sheriff Dawson was in the drivers seat and Officer Martinez in the passenger seat, both looking concerned, certainly concerned enough to warrant the flashing lights – but no sirens as it was getting to be later in the evening and they were trying not to annoy neighbours and not to pre-warn any potential criminals in the vicinity.

Both Sheriff Dawson and Officer Martinez parked on the drive outside the house. They turned the flashing light-bar off and exited their vehicle, both making furtive glances around the bushes, the trees and the house. Lisa and Jonathan rushed over to them as she said,

"Our house has been broken into and it's covered with graffiti and I mean it's everywhere!"

The local police force looked at other, nervously.

"Please folks, can you get back into your car and lock your doors, Jeffrey Walsh has escaped from Waverley House."

Forty-One

"We can't get in the car, Sandra's missing" pleaded Lisa as she looked around the area in front of and to both sides of the house. This was the worst scenario, they had already lost one daughter in the most horrific of circumstances and they couldn't face losing their only other daughter in a similar way.

Then almost as a relief, there was a loud scream, which both Lisa and Jonathan recognised as Sandra.

"YAAAAAAAAAAHHHHHHHHHH!!!!"

Both the parents looked at each other, they knew that voice.

"Oh my god, Sandra!!!" screeched Lisa and both her and Jonathan set off at pace towards the rear of the house, where the scream came from - Jonathan a few steps behind Lisa because of his leg pain and the two local police a few steps behind them, guns drawn.

As Lisa approached the corner of the house a brief sense of relief became etched on her face as she saw that her daughter was standing alone on the grass, seemingly unhurt.

Sandra was there on her own, her mouth wide open attempting to carry on her scream, but nothing was coming out. Her mouth moved, her tongue wriggled, but nothing could be heard of her 'silent scream'. She appeared to be routed to the spot, unable to move. But then she slowly and deliberately began to raise her left arm and point directly at the back of the house, which from where Lisa – and also Jonathan now at her side stood– was completely obscured from view.

As they both rounded the corner, the police force now with them too, they could see exactly what Sandra was pointing at.

Affixed to the rear of their house, ten feet up off the ground, attached to the wooden panels, was Jeffrey Walsh - naked and dead.

He was fastened to the wood with 3 ½" nails and a discarded nail gun was lying below his feet on the floor.

Hanging in a pose not dissimilar to a crucifixion, Walsh had nails through the palms of his hands; his legs were crossed, with a nail going right through them as well. The blood was still flowing from what must have been fairly recent wounds, dribbling – as opposed to gushing – down from his feet and trickling down the side of the house and splashing on the ground below.

The attack appeared to have been incredibly brutal and this was before they all looked closely at his upper torso.

Carved into his chest was Isaiah Clevedon's calling card, a deeply gouged 'I.C.' - the same as he seemed to leave on each victim's body, but this one was worse. The full stop after each letter was formed with another flat-headed nail, forced deep into either side of his sternum.

Then there was his neck, looking like a perforated line, the taught skin was a mass of roughly laid out nails going from the front around to the back, all shot in deep from the powerful tool was the nail gun, the Paslode F350S PowerMaster Plus Framing Nailer.

Moving up from his neck they all looked at his face, as Lisa pulled Sandra closer towards her, shielding her eyes from the image that would still be emblazoned in her memory forever.

Walsh's teeth had all been smashed in and the broken stumps had each been replaced with a shining stainless steel nail, glistening with fresh blood and making him look like a thing of nightmares.

Where his eyeballs used to be, the empty sockets were now home to four shiny nails in each cavernous hole, the nails penetrating the frontal part of his skull.

To top off this display of '*Tool-Time-Torture*' was the halo of nails driven into his cranium, looking like a metallic version of the 'Crown of Thorns' that Jesus had worn on the cross. Blood had left small trails - like spindly fingers - from each of the nails, across his face, over his chin and down his neck.

"Jesus Christ, we're going to have to get him down," said Sheriff Dawson out loud, as he wiped a tear from his eye, this was happening all over again and it appeared to be that bastard Clevedon's handy work once more.

Lisa put her arm around Sandra's shoulders and her and Jonathan guided her back towards the front of their home and their SUV, all climbing in and shutting the doors tight, all too stunned to utter a word. Their sanity was being wrenched away from them once more, the death of Kimmie had been very difficult to deal with, but how long was this ordeal going to continue?

Forty-Two

It was three or four hours by the time the police, ambulance and clean up guys had finished photographing, measuring, removing the body and cleaning up the mess that splattered of the back of the house.

Time itself seemed futile to the Matthews family as they tucked their now lightly sedated daughter into bed. Lisa was hoping that the five milligrams of amitriptyline that she gave to Sandra would at least quell the anguish that no doubt was coursing through her young mind. She prayed that she would sleep through the night, she thought to herself, no kid should ever have to witness such an atrocity, it was hard enough for an adult to deal with, let alone a seven-year-old child.

"Please, God, don't scar for life," Lisa said out loud.

Jonathan sat on the end of the bed, his head was heavy, and he was battling to keep his eyes from shutting, the pain in his leg had come back with a vengeance but yet he refused to take more medication. He knew he was unable to function properly as a human while on the drugs, let alone be able to protect his family. He turned to Lisa, who was pacing across the bedroom deep in thought,

"What do you suggest we do Lisa? This shit cannot continue; he is going to end up killing us all".

Lisa stopped pacing and sat on the bed beside her husband. She rested her head onto his shoulder and began to sob uncontrollably.

Jonathan wrapped his arms around his wife and kissed her on the top of her head.

"You do know I blame myself for all this, if I had never taken this job then we wouldn't be in this situation, and our beautiful Kimmie would still be with us".

Lisa was pissed off, and she turned to Jonathan. With determination in her eyes and conviction in her voice she looked at him straight and said,

"Now is not the time for self-pity, none of this is your fault it's that fucker Clevedon's fault, we are not going to let this Bastard win and our daughter die for nothing".

Jonathan was stunned by the hostility in his wife's voice but knew it was directed at Clevedon and not him. She was right, and he knew it, but still couldn't help feeling pretty fucking useless.

Both of them lay down on the bed fully clothed, with Lisa cuddling into Jonathan, and Jonathan did his best to comfort his wife. They lay in silence. None of them spoke, and the two of them closed their eyes and listened to the whistling of the wind that seeped in through the gaps of the window frame. A dog barked in the distant, its echo fading as it reached their bedroom. As they both drifted off into the land of well-deserved slumber, they dreamed.

Lisa and Jonathan sat at the table; they were both back in their pokey little flat in Boston, Lisa was finishing off reading her Agatha Christie novel 'Ten Little Niggers', while Jonathan had his head stuck firmly in the sports section of the morning paper.

Kimmie and Sandra were playing with dolls in the living room. Lisa looked up and smiled as the sound of the girl's laughter filled the room up with warmth and happiness. Kimmie walked out to the kitchen and threw her arms around Lisa and cuddled into her.

Jonathan smiled and whispered "I love you squirt" as Kimmie returned her loving gaze.

Kimmie beamed her smile back and said

"I love you, mommy, I love you, daddy, I am ok, the bad man cannot hurt me anymore".

Kimmie kissed Lisa on the cheek and whispered into her ear,

"You need to find where he is buried, mommy".

Lisa turned to look at her daughter, but she wasn't there. Sunlight crept into the bedroom through the opened curtains having little effect on the dark heaviness that swelled within the room. Jonathan was awake, and as a tear slowly filled his eye and ran down his cheek, he said to his wife –

"I dreamed about Kimmie".

Lisa sat up in bed, her hair rank with sweat clung onto her puffed out cheeks and turned to Jonathan,

"I dreamed of her too."

It was then they both realised that their recently deceased daughter had visited them in their sleep.

"We need to find where this Bastard is buried; it's the only way Jonathan".

Jonathan by now had swung his legs out the side of the bed and had pulled himself up. His leg was aching so bad and knew he had to give in and have medication. Rubbing the top of his damaged leg with the palm of his hand, he grunted in frustration at his condition,

"But how the hell are we supposed to find where his grave Lisa? It's not as if its documented on the local tour guide".

Lisa stood up and stretched the last of her sleep away.

"Sheriff Dawson will tell us, after all he was one of the guys who put him there."

With that, Lisa made her way out of the bedroom, she had to make plans but first needed a caffeine fix.

Forty-Three

Sheriff Dawson was busy typing out the report on the incident that had occurred at Eden lodge the previous evening. With each word typed, the feeling of dread gnawed at him with sharpened teeth. He knew that the secret of Isaiah Clevedon and what had happened to him some twenty years previously was about to erupt, and the proverbial shit was going to hit the fan and that he was standing directly in front of said fan. He knew that the cover-up would at least get him fired if not some prison time, but it was this that he was trying to avoid. He only had a couple of more years to retirement and he sure as shit didn't want to spend it locked up with some of the guys he ended up putting there, he knew they would make him their bitch.

****

Lisa kissed Jonathan and Sandra goodbye as she made her way to the station wagon; she was heading into town to speak to the Sheriff. She needed to make a statement about the graffiti and the corpse of Jeffery Walsh, but she also needed to find out exactly where the remains of Clevedon were.

Lisa honked the horn as the car rumbled down the dirt track towards route 15. She was both nervous and angry at the same time but knew this had to be done.

The journey into town took shorter than expected as the traffic was at a minimal. Most commuters were already at their place of work, and the roads were pretty quiet, that and the fact Lisa broke the speed limit without her even realising it, which cut the journey down by almost half.

Her first stop, when she got into town, would be the hardware store. She needed something strong enough to remove the remnants of the graffiti that the cleanup crew missed the previous night.

She pulled into the small car park just opposite the public library.

It was cold, but the rain had stayed away and only threatened the sky with its rat grey looking clouds. As she left the store, Lisa could feel everyone look at her, although they were not making it obvious she knew that a small town like this, tongues would be wagging, and sure as shit she could feel all eyes on her.

After purchasing a five-litre can of white spirits and an extra big pack of cleaning clothes, she headed back to the car, the heaviness of the can already making her fingers hurt, before heading off to see the sheriff.

Lisa pushed the door open and made her way into the police station.

It was a pokey looking place that consisted of the main entrance with four doors two either side of the counter, and another two doors at the back. She could see the Sheriff's name above the one on the right at the back. Officer Martinez was standing at the counter typing at the computer when she looked across to see Lisa.

"Hello Mrs Matthews, how are you today?"

Lisa was in no mood for small talk and thought to herself,

"*Well how the fuck would you think I am after the shit show at my place last night*", but Lisa would never say that in reality.

"Bearing up, all things considered," she said. "I need to speak to Sheriff Dawson, he is expecting me".

Officer Martinez already knew that Lisa had been expected and ushered her over to the first door on the right.

"You can go straight to his office and just knock; he will be there".

"Okay, thank you, Brandi, oh sorry Officer Martinez" she said apologetically,

"It's fine Lisa" came the officers reply.

Lisa carried on past the two desks that were situated just left of the centre of the room and headed for the Sheriff's office door. Just as she was about to knock, Sheriff Dawson opened it and greeted Lisa with a half-hearted smile.

"Mrs Matthews, I'm so glad you've found the time to come and talk to me, I promise this won't take up too much of your time."

"It's fine," Lisa said and took a seat on the adjacent chair to the Sheriff.

After fumbling about with a few pieces of paperwork, the Sheriff folded them and put them into the yellow tray opposite the computer.

"Right, first things first," he said, but Lisa was in no mood to engage in conversation about the events of last night.

"Pardon my interruption Sheriff, but I've got a few questions of my own".

Sheriff Dawson looked somewhat bemused and startled at the same time, this he was not expecting. Lisa folded her arms and sighed.

"I know all about Isaiah Clevedon, and I know exactly what happened to him and what you lot did to him, I don't care about that, what I do care about is where exactly you have buried his remains, we both know his ghost is responsible for all this shit that is occurring".

Sheriff Dawson was dumbfounded, he didn't want to believe himself that the ghost of a paedophile had somehow come back from the dead and was killing people, but all the evidence was there.

"Look Mrs Matthews, I don't know who told you what exactly, but I can assure you that its…" Before he had a chance to finish, Lisa had interrupted his speech,

"Don't give me that shit Sheriff, we both know the truth, and I think it's high time you tell me where his remains are, because you and I both know this won't end until we get his remains".

The Sheriff sat back in his chair and rocked back and forth, his stomach hung down below his shirt, and he was chewing the top of a pen.

"Okay Mrs Matthews, I will tell you everything".

He knew that it would serve nobody trying to worm out of revealing the location of where he and the others had buried Isaiah Clevedon all those years ago. Lisa sat with bated breath and an intenseness, one with which the Sheriff could only attribute to a world-class snooker player.

Once the Sheriff had finished telling Lisa the whole story behind the demise of Isaiah Clevedon, finally he revealed the resting place of the paedophile, she shuddered at the thought of his remains being so close to the lodge.

"I am not proud of what I did Mrs Matthews, but it is what it is," the sheriff said, "and despite what you may think of me, I take my role as an officer of the law very serious".

Lisa looked at the Sheriff,

"Sheriff, I for one don't blame you and nor would a million others for that matter, I would have done the same thing as you did".

The phone rang and startled Lisa. From what Lisa could gather from the phone conversation and the serious look upon Sheriff Dawson's face, something bad had happened, and she immediately thought of her husband and daughter.

"What's the matter Sheriff?" as he put the phone down he turned to Lisa,

"I am sorry Mrs Matthews, but we are going to have to leave it there for the time being."

Reluctant to say anything further to the anxious mother sat in front of him, the Sheriff got up from his chair and grabbed his hat.

"I've got to go, Mrs Matthews, something has come up."

The sheriff ushered Lisa back out to the main entrance and followed close behind her.

The Sheriff left Lisa, talking to Officer Martinez at the front desk and hurried out to his cruiser. His wife Doris had called the station and said he needed to come home quickly. Doris was unfortunate enough to have been born with the Parkinson's gene, a trait that was so kindly passed down to her by her late father and had only gotten worse these past few months, a toll that weighed heavily on the Sheriff.

The cruiser sped on past the hardware store and straight up the centre of town and out to the old Harlow road where his cottage was situated. As he turned down the narrow road leading to the front of his house he slammed on his breaks. Doris was standing in the middle of the yard, motionless and naked staring straight at the sheriff. Jeremiah knew that it was his wife, but something was different, aside from the fact she was standing naked in front of him, her eyes, her demeanour, she just looked wrong. With the engine still running, Jeremiah Dawson was poised to get out of the car, when suddenly his wife ran towards him.

"What the fuck" he said out loud as Doris ran full force into the front of the cruiser.

Her body buckled with the impact and her head rebounded off the front of the bonnet in an angry explosion of blood and broken bone. Doris got to her feet and glared at the sheriff, her eyes wide, soulless and full of pure hatred, she snarled as dribbles of foam seeped from the side of her lips. It was then he heard the voice, a thick throaty growl barked in his ear.

"Remember me, Sheriff, I fucked your niece, paybacks a bitch". Before he had a chance to reach for his gun, Isaiah Clevedon was already inside the Sheriff's body.

The cruiser door opened, and Sheriff Dawson stepped out into the haze of the afternoon sun. The grey clouds had now disbursed and had made way to clear blue skies. Doris, his wife was lying on the ground a few feet away from him, shivering in her nakedness and pleading to her husband for help. Sheriff Dawson smiled and strolled over towards her.

"Hello dear…"

Inside his mind he was trapped, held prisoner by this demon, his screams going unheard and his pleas falling on deaf ears.

He unclipped his weapon and pointed it at his wife's face. Doris tried to turn and flee but her Parkinson's had other ideas for her rendering her powerless. The crack of the gun echoed and bounced off the adjacent shed to the house.

Crows, who were nesting in nearby treetops squawked in terror as they flapped frantically and took flight. Doris Dawson's naked body lay on her back, wisps of wind curled up around the clumps of matted hair and lumps of brain, coating it lightly in a blanket of dust. Her husband stood over her watching, grinning, as blood seeped out from the gaping hole where her face used to be.

Coldness suddenly gripped Jeremiah shocking him back to reality. Isaiah Clevedon had left his body. Sheriff Dawson fell to his knees, still holding his gun as the shock took its hold. Tilting his head back and staring towards the blue sky above, he whispered the name of his beloved Doris, and as the last syllable departed his dry cracked lips he pulled the trigger one last time. The gun dropped from his fingers and fell to the ground as the body of Jeremiah Dawson slumped sideways beside his dead wife. The darkness retreated into the shadows and disappeared.

Forty-Four

After leaving the police station, Lisa made her way back to the car.

A sudden feeling of dread seemed to enclose around her as she sat, staring out of the window. The sun was saying goodbye to the day as it began to set, slowly casting colours of deep orange and amber onto the rooftops of the nearby buildings.

She was content with the information she had gotten off the Sheriff, but what she would do with it, she didn't know. What she did know was that she wasn't going down without a fight. Isaiah Clevedon could rot in hell, where he belonged. After a couple of minutes daydreaming, Lisa turned the key in the ignition; it took a couple of tries before the old Volkswagen coughed into life belching out a plume of black smoke from its exhaust. Lisa's mind flooded with thoughts of her deceased daughter.

The drive back to the lodge took longer than expected, due to a broken down lorry at the start of route 15, and the road going down to one lane for traffic. The temperature inside the old car was reading seventy, but Lisa still felt a chill to her bones. She was exhausted and hungry but didn't feel she would be able to manage much to eat. As she drew closer and closer to the broken lorry, Lisa could see Brandi Martinez ushering traffic on two at a time. She stood waving the cars forward, two big wet patches of sweat had formed on the officers blue shirt, under her armpits, and every so often she would wipe her forehead with the back of her hand. Sheriff Dawson was nowhere to be seen.

Lisa pulled the handbrake on and put the car in neutral, officer Martinez signaled at her to roll down the window, which Lisa happily obliged. Brandi leaned on the opened car window and hung her head down to reach eye level with Lisa.

"Hi, Lisa" came the officer's croaky voice.

Lisa guessed that the constant flow of smog and exhaust fumes was playing havoc on the officer's chest. A cold breeze wafted in through the opened window, and Lisa caught a good whiff of stale sweat emanating from the officer and had to swallow, or she would have ended up gagging.

"I've been trying to get hold of the Sheriff, but he is not answering his radio" Brandi said in a concerned voice, "have you seen him since he left the station earlier?"

Lisa coughed and swallowed the lump of phlegm that oozed into her mouth,

"No, I'm sorry, I've not seen him", Lisa said.

"Okay not to worry, I am sure he has good reason not to answer the radio, this traffic is a nightmare."

"It sure is Lisa said."

"The tow truck is on its way, should be here within the hour, I will radio the sheriff again once this lot is moving freely again".

Lisa just nodded in agreement.

"Have a safe journey home Mrs Matthews."

"Thank you," Lisa said before winding up the window once more, and glad that she no longer had to smell the stale sweat of a burly police officer. Once Lisa had passed the lorry, she was able to get out of second gear and make her way home.

Forty-Five

As Lisa drove off into the distance her car disappearing over the hill, Brandi Martinez continued to conduct the traffic, keeping the flow moving steadily, waving the cars on with her white gloved hands.

She had been standing there in this spot for the last hour and the chances of the lorry being removed from the scene still seemed like a long time off.

As the cars slowly passed by, all the drivers and passengers were 'rubber-necking' to see what was happening. The temperature was still in the mid-70's as the afternoon dragged on and the shift for Brandi seemed to drag on even longer, due to feeling a little overcome by the heat, the thickness of her uniform and temperature radiating up from the already hot and sticky tarmac.

The lorry had broken down just over an hour and half before, Brandi getting the call to the scene a half hour after the initial breakdown. The driver had pulled the lorry over as close to the side of the road as he could and because of being parked slightly on the edge of the road, the vehicle was parked precariously at an angle, but was still allowing a single line of traffic to slowly pass by.

The driver - Martin Hammett - had been standing at the side of the lorry, on the grass verge for the duration, since he'd parked up. He'd rang his company for back up and for them to arrange a tow truck to arrive and take him and his vehicle - a large 18 wheeler - back to the depot.

Standing at the side of the road, drinking a small bottle of Dr. Pepper and eating a sandwich that he found in his cab, behind a stack of CD's that he'd just bought the day before, Hammett was soaking up the sun rays as he stood playing the waiting game, nothing happening, nothing occurring.

"How long did they tell you they'd be?" asked Brandi as she sidled up to the trucker, smiling her best 'law enforcement officer' smile.

"They didn't say, they just said something about '*as soon as they can'*."

Cars were still passing by, most of them slowing down as they passed the vehicle to see what was happening.

"Move along folks, nothing to see here" shouted Brandi, waving the cars past and making herself even hotter from her rapid arm movements.

One car drove past, their stereo blasting a loud song, guitars blaring, drums pounding. Brandi scratched her head, just at the moment this car drove past, the sun went behind a cloud, the temperature dropped and all the area around the slow moving cars and the stranded lorry were plunged into near darkness. The atmosphere turned decidedly 'spooky' and Brandi looked at the 18 wheel vehicle behind her and for a split second, a fraction of time, a miniscule moment - she could have sworn that she saw Isaiah Clevedon, the bane of her life, sat in the drivers seat of the cab laughing.

"What's that song playing?" Brandi asked Hammett as she wiped a few dripping beads of sweat from her brow.

"Oh that's 'Sympathy for the Devil' by the Stones" he replied.

"How appropriate," she replied looking at the lorry again and now seeing no one in there at the wheel.

"Whatcha mean?" asked Hammett.

"Nothing, it's not important…"

Then all hell broke loose…

There was a cracking and creaking noise and before Brandi could move the lorry began to topple over sideways, heading towards her.

Her feet wouldn't move and as the lorry starting tipping towards her, for a brief moment in time she saw Clevedon once more. Sitting in the cab laughing out loud. She thought to herself –

"*Why can't no one else hear this? Why has he selected me? Why am I the on…*"

The lorry hit her like a small landslide on a mountain, taking out a village and obliterating it - which was exactly what happened to Officer Brandi Martinez, ex-Police Officer of the Martha's Vineyard Police Department.

As the lorry leant onto her with all its weight, their was an incredibly loud 'popping' noise as the full force of the 18-Wheeler crushed her torso and split her sides wide open. The continued pressure pushed all of her organs out onto the warm tarmac road painting the area red and within a fraction of a second the cab swung around and made its descent onto her as well.

As she lay their pinned under the chassis of the vehicle, the driver's cab came closer and closer until eventually making contact with her head. As the mass of steel pushed down on her cranium all she could hear one final time was Isaiah Clevedon's laughing intermingled with the Stones still playing a distance away down the road.

"*How bloody appropriate…*" were her final thoughts as the lorry crushed her skull into the gritty blood soaked road, cracking her head open and bursting her brains and more blood out of her smashed head, pouring the contents, splashing and spurting all over the ground.

Forty-Six

Lisa pulled up outside their home.

As she exited the car once more on their driveway, she had a feeling that 'closure' would never happen. This job had been a godsend when Jonathan had been successful at interview, but from taking up residence at Eden Lodge, their lives had definitely not been so good.

Jonathan had taken it very badly and felt that all of the incidents were his fault – the loss of Kimmie, the death of Ronnie and Jeffrey and the near permanent damage to his leg, it was almost too much to take. Their dream job and home was not turning out the way that they had hoped it would.

Walking up the steps, Lisa looked at her home, from the outside it looked perfect, beautifully presented and beyond anything they could have dreamt of when still living in the city, but just look at it now. As she opened the door she was still greeted with stains on walls where the graffiti had been; the majority of the paintwork had been removed by the 'clean-up-crew', but if you looked closely you could still see slight marks of where it once was. It was lucky that she had gone to the hardware store and picked up the cleaning products, but she'd be busy for a long time taking the worst of the remainder of the paint off.

Jonathan laying on the sofa trying to relax in front of the TV with Sandra, cuddled up watching an old 'Black & White' comedy film. Rex was also curled up next to them on the sofa, snoozing in the patch of afternoon sun that was shining in from the window and landing directly on his back, warming him up in the process.

She decided to leave them to it and headed towards the stairs.

"I won't be too long, I'm going upstairs to have a shower; all behave yourselves."

"Don't we always?" replied Jonathan, waving to Lisa over his shoulder whilst rubbing Sandra's head with his other hand.

"Mmmmmm…" she said as she made her way up the stairs to the bathroom.

Walking along the hallway Lisa kept glimpsing something just out of view, at the corner of her peripheral vision and then it was gone again, happening several times as she went into the bathroom to start the shower running, drop her clothes into the wicker basket in her bedroom and when she walked back to the bathroom, wrapped just in a towel.

The temperature dropped once more and Lisa could tell that something 'supernatural' was about to take place once again, the prelude to a vision was becoming more and more obvious and her nerves were a little less on edge.

As she stood in the bathroom she looked at the mirror and lettering gradually appeared in the condensation, a message from the 'other side'.

'He…is…on…his…way…here…again…'

Standing staring at the message she knew who it was from as she recognised the handwriting, it was Kimmie's.

A message from beyond the grave from her daughter, she wiped the tears from her eyes as she prepared herself for what might happen.

Forty-Seven

Jonathan sat at the kitchen table with his head in his hands; he was thinking about Kimmie and how he blamed himself for her death. A father was supposed to protect his children, but he had failed. Lisa sat opposite while Sandra was busy drawing in the living room.

"You can't blame yourself, Jonathan, it was not our fault, it was that Bastards doing, he was the one who took our precious Kimmie away from us".

Jonathan's leg was aching, but his heart was aching even more to take much notice of the dull pain that meandered up to his ribs. Lisa turned to look at Sandra, the paper she was drawing on lay on the floor, but Sandra was not there. Lisa thought that she must be watching TV, but she could hear no sound coming from the room. She went in to make sure she was okay.

A sudden iciness festered in the air, Lisa could see her breath evaporate with every exhale. She tried to scream but whatever had hold of her physical being was preventing her, she was frozen to the spot.

Sandra was stood by the window glaring outwards towards the woods, her head turned towards Lisa, her eyes, black, lifeless and vacant, bore deep into Lisa's very soul. Lisa still could not move. Red marks suddenly appeared across her daughters face, and still, Sandra stood staring at her mother. The marks began to weep as they became deeper and deeper, blood streamed down both cheeks of her daughters face, but the scratches had a pattern to them. The initials I.C were carved by an invisible hand in great red angry looking slices, across both cheeks of Lisa's daughter.

Somewhere, somehow, Lisa found enough strength to scream. Her shrill blood-curdling cry's jolted Jonathan from the kitchen table, and in three great strides, he limped into where his wife and daughter were.

"What the fuck", Jonathan roared, "No you don't, not again, leave my daughter alone you fucker."

But it was no good, as Jonathan began to scramble across the room towards his daughter, a sudden volt of electricity shot through his body, his fingers gripped the walking cane like a vice, every muscle in his whole body flexed with the pain. His hair, burnt and smouldering made him feel nauseous, but the electricity rendered him useless. Both Lisa and Jonathan could only watch as their possessed daughter floated up into the air and disappeared in a shower of broken glass out through the window and into the woods.

The lights within the room flickered, Jonathan and Lisa stood frozen at that moment in time. Their chests on fire and their hearts pounding. The light appeared just to the right of Lisa. A figure appeared from within the glow, then another. Hyacinth and Emily stood in front of the living and held hands. A beam of bright iridescent light surrounded Sandra's parents, and the feeling of warmth and pure love, coursed through their already battered bodies. Jonathan fell to the floor with a thud, while Lisa held on to the couch to steady herself. The figures had disappeared, and they both had feeling again in their bodies.

Lisa ran to her husband and helped him to his feet. His fingers were charred black, but he was able to move, albeit slowly. They both knew they had to go and get their daughter, Jonathan was not going to let his remaining child perish by the hands of this devil, busted leg or not. Thanks to Jeremiah Dawson, they knew exactly where to find Sandra.

Lisa grabbed two coats that were hanging on the back of the kitchen door.

Both of them were scared, but the determination and love for their daughter outweighed any fear they had. With her arm around her husband's waist, they both headed out towards the woods and to the pit where they would find the remains of Isaiah Clevedon.

Outside, thick black clouds spread across the skyline, the sun's rays doing little to penetrate the blanket of black. The wind had picked up, and there was a distinct chill in the air. They both went into the heaviness of the thick undergrowth of the forest. After a couple of minutes, Jonathan had to stop to rest for a short while. His leg throbbed and his fingers hurt, he knew that he would lose at least a couple of them, but that was not his concern at that moment.

"Jonathan, are we going to get our daughter back?"

Jonathan turned to face his wife who was now sitting beside him on one of the downed trees, a casualty of the passing storm.

"No mother should ever have to say those words, Lisa, as God is my witness, we will get our Sandra back".

Lisa tried to force a believing smile, but it had little effect on their states of minds.

"Come on, we need to get going," Jonathan said as he leaned on his wife's shoulder for support.

****

After another twenty or so minutes, that felt like twenty hours, Jonathan pointed in the direction of the little clearing that he had stumbled upon a few weeks earlier.

"Over there, Lisa, that's where we will find Sandra."

Lisa, with her arm firmly wrapped around Jonathan's waist, trudged on through the flailing arms of the trees to where their daughter was.

As they got to the edge of the clearing, they could see Sandra lying beside a disturbed mound of dirt and soil. She looked lifeless, and Lisa prayed that they were not too late. The wind howled through the trees as it blew dead branches and debris up into the air. That is when they saw it. Standing three foot away from their daughter was this black shadow, a mass, looming over the little girl. Its shape not distinct and its blackness seemed to shape-shift. They knew it was him.

Jonathan rested against the side of a wilting redwood, his energy and gone from zero to nothing and was unable to walk anymore.

"Lisa, be careful, I think he is draining me, you will have to get Sandra".

Exhausted and in severe pain, Jonathan passed out.

"Shit," Lisa said as she kneeled by her husband.

The black mass seemed to be moving around the outline of the clearing, getting further and further away from Sandra. Lisa saw her chance and sprinted towards her daughter. Before she knew it, the black mass had taken shape; the ghost of Isaiah Clevedon stood directly opposite Lisa and her daughter. Its grotesque laugh seemed to ricochet off every tree and was amplified by the howling wind. Lisa leaned over her daughter to protect her from this thing, this evil.

The ground began to shake violently, branches snapped and hurled towards the pine carpeted forest floor. Lisa prayed with all her heart as the mound of raised dirt began to crack like an egg. The rusted bodywork of an old Volkswagen appeared from beneath the soil. Its windows, shattered, broken and it's hole rusted frame bent in the middle causing the roof to slant forward, and its faded green paint encrusted with the brownish stains of twenty years beneath the soil. A mound of dirty sodden clothes, lay spread across the front seats with the bones of its owner staring back at Lisa in an ominous deathly stare. Lisa knew it was

Isaiah. Cradling her daughter in her arms, Lisa cried and called out to her god,

"Please dear God, don't let this evil take another daughter".

Isaiah screamed, its howl shaking the very bones of Lisa as it made its way towards her. Looking up as the entity's blackness loomed over her, Lisa gasped. Out of nowhere two bright lights suddenly appeared. Four small hands, two either side of the blackness reached out and grabbed it, like an eternal tug of war. The ghosts of Emily and Hyacinth had hold of Isaiah Clevedon.

Emily turned towards Lisa and in a whispered voice said,

"Go we can't hold him for long".

Lisa swept her daughter up in both arms and ran towards Jonathan who was coming too by the edge of the clearing. Jonathan stood up by the tree and eased himself back into reality.

Lisa ran towards him and screamed.

"Come on Jonathan, find the strength, we have to go, NOW!"

Jonathan's jaw dropped as he gazed at the Phantom. He quickly grabbed his cane and held on to his wife as the three of them fumbled their way through the thick forest and back towards the lodge. A couple of times Jonathan had lost his footing and went head first onto the ground, but he quickly and surprisingly got straight up and carried on with his family.

Lisa, Jonathan and their daughter reached the lodge.

The air inside was damp with the coldness that lingered outside. As the three of them entered the hallway, Jonathan closed the door and locked it. He wasn't sure what good if any, locking the door would achieve, but he did it anyway. Sandra whimpered as she felt the deep cuts to her face,

"Its ok sweetheart, we will fix you right up", Lisa said.

Sandra looked exhausted. After attending to the wounds on her daughter's face and laying her down in her bed for some rest, Lisa turned her attention to her husband. By now, the pain in his hands was rife, and Lisa could do little, but bandage them in a damp towel. Lisa took her husband's badly blistered face in her hands and kissed the top of his head,

"We got her back" she said, "We got her back".

Both of them held one another and rested their heads on each other's shoulders. Lisa closed her eyes and drifted off into a daydream.

Lisa and both of the girls were on the beach in Miami; it was only their second ever holiday together as a family. The sun was beaming down, and Kimmie and Sandra were playing by the water's edge. The sea, with its gentle blue-green waves, caressed the tip of the beach as they broke, it's sound almost hypnotic.

Lisa watched as her daughters played gracefully; they were happy. Her husband had wandered off to fetch ice cream for the four of them and was on his way back. Lisa smiled as Jonathan's toned body came into view; he was a handsome man.

The screams ripped through the quietness of the lodge. Lisa jerked her eyes opened and gasped as both her and Jonathan realised they had drifted off.

Both of them in unison looked at each other and screamed "Sandra".

Jonathan being the slower of the two, told Lisa to run and run quick. Lisa shot up from her husbands, loving grasp and ascended the stairs two steps at a time. As she reached the last step, the air surrounding her was cold, ice cold. She knew that it was back. Lisa scrambled for her daughter's bedroom.

The black mass enveloped the entire ceiling, its ominous shape reaching out at Sandra as she lay paralysed in a state of fear on her bed. Tears streamed down her young face and eyes, as red as the devil himself peered at her, burned a hole deep into her soul. As the mass loomed forward, it engulfed Sandra's entire body. Her eyes, now flickering with just the whites rolled up to the back of their sockets. Her whole body jerked and twitched in a violent spasm as the entity of the paedophile began ravaging her body, just like he had done with her sister.

Lisa screamed,

"Leave her alone, you bastard" as Jonathan struggled to get to his feet.

Pain shot up through his body like a million stabbing needles, his face contorted and grimaced with searing pain, and Lisa could only watch on as her husband was thrown violently into the wardrobe. The timber cracked and splintered, piercing Jonathans back. Fresh warm blood seeped from the gaping wound rendering him useless and unable to move. But the ghost of Isaiah Clevedon was not done with the girl's father yet.

Blackness surrounded Jonathan and seeped into every pore of his already weakened body. His arms outstretched and his remaining fingers bent back at right angles, cracked as each digit snapped. His body, heavy and cumbersome remained pinned to the back wall.

Lisa watched on in complete horror as her husband's body began to slide up towards the ceiling. His leg, the one that had been stitched by the hospital, became taut as each of the stitches unravelled and split, revealing the hole where the tree had snagged him. Bone snapped off in his leg like a twig, tore from him with the invisible force of blackened hands. Jonathan squealed, the desperation in his face evident to his crying wife.

Lisa helplessly watched on as her remaining daughter's body began to buck in mid-air and float above the bed; she was powerless to help. A wind, so powerful swept through the bedroom like a tornado, sending teddy bears and bed covers flying, then, from the far side of the bedroom, a light began to emerge. It was dull at first, and Lisa didn't know where it was coming from, it was barely visible but started to grow stronger and brighter until its light was almost too much to bear. Lisa covered her eyes as the light began to take form, a shape that she recognised, stood translucent and held within an aura.

Lisa cried as she could see the ghostly figure of her recently deceased daughter Kimmie standing alongside two other figures. Kimmie looked over at her mother and smiled, her voice, distorted and seemed distant spoke to her,

"It's okay mommy."

Tears blinded Lisa as she struggled to comprehend exactly what she was bearing witness too. Lisa wept as her dead daughter moved towards the bed that her sister was on.

Kimmie, Emily and Hyacinth, circled Sandra and the entity of Isaiah Clevedon. The three girls held hands and closed their eyes. White light exploded from the three ghosts, a shower of beaming light exploded and shot through the young body of Sandra. The black mass, with its deep demonic growl, screamed at the girls, its eyes burning redder than lava, tore holes into the streams of light that were emanating from all three of the girls, but their light remained strong, and soon the blackness was suffocating, it's grotesque shape scratched at the air as light tore through its darkness.

Sandra's weakened body landed on the bed with a thud. Lisa, through her love for her daughter, dived onto the bed and grabbed her into her arms. She held her head close to her chest and sobbed. Blood from the wounds on Sandra's cheeks, soaked into her mothers white top staining it a cloudy red. Sandra came too and gazed at the apparitions of her sister and her two friends, Emily and Hyacinth. All three transparent girls smiled as they surrounded the bed.

Lisa reached out her hand to Kimmie and whispered the words "*I love you*" to her daughter. Kimmie smiled back at her mother.

The entity of Isaiah Clevedon squirmed within its blackness; its eyes were depicting hatred as it fought against the light that was drowning him, it's evil, swirling around in circles grasping its devilish fingers in an attempt to grab at Sandra and her mother.

Kimmie, Emily and Hyacinth's light glowed brighter than ever.

Jonathan groaned as he stirred within the broken timbers, his body too badly hurt from the impact to stand up.

Isaiah Clevedon snarled from within its blackness, sending the room into a violent windswept tornado, sucking at the mother and daughter as they huddled together for safety. Jonathan could only watch as the spirit of his dead daughter fought against the malevolence of the dead paedophile.

Sandra and Lisa slid from the bed to the floor, their strength all but sucked dry from the entities within the room, and finding it harder and harder to resist the power of the wind. Angry gusts swirled around above their heads, the blackness embroiled with the light from the three girls, ripping plasterboard and timbers from the ceiling and throwing them in every direction.

Sandra's 'Frozen' lamp shot out from the turmoil and smashed on the wall beside Jonathan's head, showering him in tiny shards of bulb and splintered porcelain. Jonathan called to his wife,

"Lisa, crawl over to me."

Lisa raised her head and saw Jonathan who was leaning up against the back wall. Still clutching her daughter she crawled along the bedroom floor towards her husband. Jonathan leaned forward, reaching out his hand to Lisa.

"Almost there Lisa" he screamed, his voice barely audible above the noise of the battle that overhead.

Isaiah Clevedon's growl resonated off the walls as he began to succumb to the intense light from the three ghosts.

Jonathan grabbed his wife's hand and with every ounce of energy he had left, dragged the two of them towards him.

Lisa, Sandra and Jonathan gripped on to each other and closed their eyes. Lisa pressed Sandra's head in towards her body to shield her from the madness that was going on around them. With one final immense spark, the windows shattered, showering the bed with a million fragments of glass, and the darkness that was Isaiah Clevedon was no more.

****

Lisa watched from the kitchen window with a smile as Sandra played in the garden with Rex the cat.

She glanced over at the clock on the wall and realised that her husband would be home soon from his job as the administrative manager for Eden Lodge, a job that was offered by the company in remittance for the injuries that he had sustained six months earlier, that along with twenty thousand dollars helped with some of the stress involved with rebuilding their lives.

Up above, footsteps tiptoed across the wooden floorboards leading out from Kimmie's old room. This brought happiness to this once darkened home.

Every so often Lisa would catch a split-second glimpse of a little girl in a white dress; this warmed her heart although her little family were still recovering from the nightmare of Isaiah Clevedon and would be for some time.

The door opened, and Jonathan stood smiling at his beautiful wife, a fresh bunch of carnations that were on the window, gently swayed in the afternoon's breeze filtered their scented aroma in the air.

Lisa smiled at her husband as he made his way towards her. He still walked with a limp, and he was getting used to having only three fingers on his left hand, but life was better, scars heal, but memories never fade, as they say.

THE END

Printed in Great Britain
by Amazon

35848261R00112

Ian Carroll is a best selling author, with all of his books available on Amazon in paperback and also on Kindle.

Ian is the author of the 'A-Z of Bloody Horror' books, which feature among its titles – ***'Warning: Water May Contain Mermaids'***, ***'Antique Shop'***, ***'Clown in Aisle 3'*** *and* ***'Pensioner'***. Also the author of the horror books ***'My Name is Ishmael'***, ***'Demon Pirates Vs. Vikings – Blackhorn's Revenge'***, ***'The Lover's Guide to Internet Dating'*** *and* ***'Valentines Day'***.
Ian is also the author of many Music Books including the '***Fans Have Their Say***' series and Official Book of the Reading Festival (UK).

Ian lives with his wife Raine, two sons – Nathan & Josh - plus Stanley and the memories of a jet-black witches cat called Rex - in Plymouth, Devon, UK.

Paddy is a 41-year-old author/singer/songwriter, who has a passion for writing, and whose weapon of choice is clearly the pen.

Paddy hails from Dublin, but is firmly rooted here in Plymouth.
He has five children, Regan, Shauna, Lilianna, Coby and Freya, which keeps him on his toes.

He is the author of '***Plymouth, a War in Words***', which is dedicated to the history of the 'Ocean City' in which he resides. Paddy is an avid writer of all things poetical and macabre and has many poems and short stories published to his name.
Paddy's mind is a mesh of King, Herbert and Koontz all rolled into one big ball of horrific fiction and is compelled to give anybody a scare.

Carroll and Mullen, the new names in Horror.

ISBN - 9781672017510

Phantoms

'There is something in the woods...'